Regret

Never Waste a Second Chance

JANICE M. WHITEAKER

Regret, Book 2 of the Never Waste a Second Chance series

Copyright 2016 by Janice M. Whiteaker
www.janicemwhiteaker.com

All rights reserved. No part of this publication may be reproduced, stored in a retrieval system, or transmitted in any form or by any means electronic, mechanical, photocopying, recording, or otherwise without the prior written permission of the publisher and copyright owner except for the use of brief quotations in a book review.

First printing, 2016

Cover design by Robin Harper at Wicked by Design.
Editing by Laura Seroka.

*For my husband,
because a little peice of him is in every book I write.*

Sorry if that grosses you out.

ONE

PAUL FOUGHT THE urge to jump as a sharp pinch stung his left ass cheek for the fourth time in under a half hour. The already irritated flesh ached with what would certainly be an angry bruise as he quickly descended the ladder hoping to take the advantage away from the tiny, hunched woman standing below him.

His work boots hit the ground and he darted away from the fingers, gnarled with arthritis, already headed his way. Hazel giggled like a schoolgirl, her pale blue eyes glimmering under lids heavy with age. Paul sighed.

"That's the last one." He folded the six-foot ladder he kept in his old truck, being careful not to give his ex-girlfriend's mother any openings. He unhooked the plastic bag over his arm that held ten burned out light bulbs and held it out to the old woman.

She took the bag from him and batted her eyes. "What would I do without you Paulie?"

His aggravation with her good-natured flirting softened. "Call me anytime. I don't want you to get hurt again trying to change these on your own." He looked up at the soaring ceilings in the old house. It was a miracle she hadn't been hurt worse.

She dismissed his concern with a wave of her hand. "Takes more than a little spill to off an old wiry bat like me." Hazel shuffled in the direction of the kitchen, her pink terry cloth slippers barely making a sound as she moved across the thin-planked hardwood floors. "Let me get my purse darlin'."

Paul let the ladder angle down until it was parallel with the floor before hooking it under his arm. "You know I'm not taking any money from you."

The old woman turned and put her hands on her hips, tucking the volume of her housecoat against the slightness of her frame. "You come all the way over here, change my lights and fix my toilet." Her heavily drawn on eyebrows wiggled across the lines of her forehead. "All while I have my wicked way with you. It's the least I can do."

Paul followed behind her as she continued on in search of the black synthetic leather handbag he knew darn well was sitting on her bedside table. "I live one block over and it took me all of a half hour. I'm happy to do it if it keeps you from standing on a coffee table sitting on a dining room table and attempting it yourself."

Hazel dropped the bag of spent bulbs onto the yellowed kitchen counter and crossed her arms, her mauve lips drawing into a tight line. "I'm still so mad at her."

Paul eyed the door. With the ladder he was almost as wide as he was tall so the chance of being able to make a quick escape was less than zero. She had him trapped, just like at the top of the ladder, only this time she was coming at him with something way worse that those two surprisingly strong fingers.

"That man she has now is worthless. No job, no skills, no sense of humor." Hazel shook her head, the crisp nearly white curls covering it still as stone. "Worthless."

The word settled in his gut like one too many servings of dumplings. Heavy and sickening.

Worthless.

The man he was left for was worthless. The man a woman chose over him. The man she carried on with behind his back.

It shouldn't sting like it did. He hadn't loved her, no matter how hard he tried. Maybe that was why, no matter how good he was to a woman, how well he treated her, she always left, usually for someone else, someone who claimed they loved her.

Hazel slid a slim white cigarette out of a hard pack she grabbed off the counter. Squeezing it between her lips, she flicked an amber lighter to life and sucked in, the pursing of her mouth transferring lipstick onto the filtered end. As she slowly blew the smoke out, Hazel shook her head again. "She picked wrong. I told her that too." She took another draw. "Probably why I don't see her much."

He didn't want to have this conversation before and he didn't want to have it now, but the idea that an old woman was risking her relationship with her daughter over incorrect assumptions would eat him up. "She made the right choice. I didn't love her."

Hazel's already thin lips flattened even more. She flung the hand holding her cigarette to one side. "What's love?" She leaned back against the counter her face a mix of aggravation and disbelief. "What does it matter if a man says he loves you when he's a worthless piece of shit?"

Paul could answer that question.

A lot. It matters a lot.

Her daughter wasn't the first to leave him over the only four-letter word he'd ever had a hard time saying, but he did decide she would be the last. "Don't hold it against her. She just wanted someone to love her." Paul edged toward the door.

"What about you?" The softness in Hazel's voice surprised him. She was bawdy and brutally honest and he'd liked her from the get-go, but she herself struggled with the softer emotions. Maybe that's why they got along.

He backtracked, siding up to her small frame, being careful not to clear the kitchen shelf with the ladder. "I got you." He leaned down and planted a kiss on her soft cheek.

The blush coloring her face was still blooming as he pulled the door closed, taking full advantage of her momentary silence to make a hasty retreat before she found more uncomfortable things to talk about.

The ladder was loaded up and he was idling at the only stop sign between his house and Hazel's when he had an idea. Maybe he could get her set up with a local church. Have the ladies go out and keep her company. They'd probably even bring her lunch.

The thought was short lived. The image of her sitting around with the church ladies, smoking and cussing as they sat wide-eyed, saying silent prayers for her salvation, was enough to make him laugh out loud. He was still chuckling when he pulled into the lot at the hardware store.

It was crunch time on the house he and the boss lady were renovating. Now Mina was more of a partner, and she hated being called boss, but any opportunity to aggravate her, was an opportunity he happily took.

They were almost out of drywall screws and Paul was doing his damndest to make sure the job stayed stocked. If he and Mina had any hope of finishing their current job before ground broke on rebuilding Thomas' house there couldn't be any delays, no matter how small.

His mood immediately sobered, all amusement and thoughts of Hazel gone. The wind whipped around him as he hurried across the blacktop, hands tucked in the pockets of his heavy canvas coat, doing his best to ignore the stab in his gut.

That damn house.

He could hardly stand to think of it. When that place burned down it could have taken people with it. People who were important to him. Thomas. Mina.

Nancy.

The icy wind pulled the air from his lungs. That's what he told himself anyway, even though it took more than a few seconds inside the warmth of the store to get it back.

"You like it here so far?"

Paul recognized the voice and it made him consider walking back out the door, but he'd never been one to walk away from an asshole. And he needed a box of goddamned screws.

He passed the desk knowing his presence wouldn't go unnoticed. A six-four, two-hundred and fifty pound frame was hard to hide, but he was going to try anyway. The less he had to deal with him the better.

"Paul!" Mike's voice called out the minute he came into view. It had been more than a few months since he'd seen his old classmate and Paul could swear the man was even fatter and his hair dyed even blacker, if either of those was even possible. "Come over here. I want you to meet someone."

The man standing next to Mike was about the same age, but that was where the similarities ended. He was tall. Not as tall as Paul, but significantly taller than Mike. He was lean, probably could still wear the pants he wore in college. He had all his hair, cropped close to the sides of his head in what Paul could only imagine was a trendy style. He was tan. In early March. The coldest early March in as long as Paul could remember.

"This is Neil. New owner." Mike thumbed in Paul's direction. "This is my buddy Paul. You'll see him a lot."

Paul decided not to correct Mike on the 'my buddy' part. He held his hand out to Neil. "Nice to meet you."

Neil took his hand in a shake that told Paul everything he needed to know about the guy. Limp wrist, weak squeeze. Just like Mike. A man who tried like hell to look the part, but when it came down to it his sack didn't take up nearly enough space in his boxers.

"Neil just moved here from Iowa. Got divorced and wanted a change." Mike ran a meaty hand over his slick comb-over.

Neil leaned back against the counter at his back. "I needed some fresh meat. Gotta find the next Mrs. Meyers."

Yup. This guy was exactly what Paul thought. A turd.

"Good luck with that." Paul turned to leave before he said something he'd regret. This was the closest hardware store by quite a few miles and he didn't want his mouth to ruin it for him.

"I was telling Neil there were quite a few opportunities in town I'd like to get my hands on, right Paul?"

Paul froze. Closing his eyes, he took a deep breath. Every damn time he saw Mike it ended the same way. Mike's married ass talking about all the women he wanted to get his fat fuckin' paws on. Paul's feet were moving toward the front of the store before this situation could go any further. Turned out walking away was much easier sober. He'd get the screws tomorrow. Somewhere else.

He barely made it to the door before Mike's voice rang out behind him, loud enough it was clear he intended to be heard. "You'll have to check out Nancy Richards. She's a hot piece I'll tell ya that. Just needs a real man to make her see what she's been missing out on."

There were few things he wanted to do more than turn around and punch Mike right in his bloated face. Lucky for Mike one of those things would make that a counterproductive move.

He pushed back out into the cold night air and forced his feet to keep moving until he was back in his truck driving toward his last stop of the evening. Hopefully, it went better than the last.

If not, it could bring a swift end to nearly three months of sobriety.

His blood was still pumping hot in his veins as he parked the truck outside the auto parts storefront. A quick trip in and he'd have a new battery for his girl and head home to spend the evening getting her back up and running.

It took him less than two minutes to grab what he needed and be at the empty checkout counter. He leaned across, checking to see if someone was crouched down going through the manuals lining the shelving under the registers. No luck.

He was about to dump the battery and call the night a loss when the sound of voices from the far side of the store made him pause. He stalked toward them.

"Can I get someone to check me ou--" His words died in his throat.

"Hi Paul." Nancy stood next to a store employee easily ten years younger, six different wiper blades in her hands. She shifted on her feet.

"Hi Nan." It was all he could manage. Sadly it was better than what he usually came up with when she was around.

She looked down at the slim, clam-shelled packages. "I'm sorry for holding you up. I needed new wiper blades and I was trying to figure out which ones to get." She turned to the man standing behind her and then back again, oblivious to the daggers he was shooting Paul's direction. "He was helping me."

The man cleared his throat. "I'll be with you in a minute sir." His eyes went back to Nancy.

Paul stepped forward, snagged the blades for Nancy's Honda off the shelf and held them up. "Got 'em."

Nancy slid the wipers she held back into place before reaching for the set Paul held. "Thank you."

He tucked them under his arm alongside the battery. "I got it." He turned and went back to the counter, setting his battery and Nancy's wipers on the glass surface.

Another employee came out of nowhere and greeted him with a smile. "Did you find everything okay?"

"Yup."

The man yammered on as he finished the transaction, but none of it registered. His brain was focused completely on the woman standing close by his side. So close he could smell her perfume, and it was not at all what he expected. It was different than anything he'd ever smelled. It was exotic. It was spicy. It was sweet.

It was perfectly fitting and it was ruining his already shitty night.

Receipt in hand, Paul left the store, holding the door open for a very quiet Nancy. She followed him into the lot, her brows drawn together. They grew even closer, a worry line forming in the middle, as they walked past his truck.

He set the battery by her front tire and snapped open the first wiper pack. Before he could get the old blade off, she was at his side.

"You don't have to do this. I can have Thomas do it tomorrow."

He snapped open the second pack. "It's already almost done."

Nancy huffed out a breath, the puff of hot air hanging like a filmy cloud in the air between them. She grabbed around inside her purse. "Well you certainly didn't need to pay for them." She yanked her wallet free and unsnapped it, flipping the leather case open. "Let me at least pay you back."

"No." The word came out harsher than he meant it but maybe that was a good thing.

Grabbing the trash and old blades along with his new battery, Paul stepped away from the car and away from her, but he made the mistake of not turning away.

She stood beside the car, wallet still clutched in her hand, looking oddly defeated. "The engagement party is tomorrow. Are you coming?"

He shook his head, knowing his answer wasn't going to come as a surprise. He'd told the bride-to-be he wasn't coming a dozen times. "Can't."

She stared at him, her mouth barely opening before closing tightly shut.

He wanted to stay just a few seconds more, looking at her. Watching her silky blonde hair flip with the wind, her cheeks turning pink from the cold. Watching her watching him, but that was one more thing that would be a counterproductive move.

He had a life to live and there was only one way he could do it and still keep his sanity.

"Goodbye Nan."

TWO

NANCY CAUGHT HER hip on the edge of the white Formica counter topping the center island as she hurried around the kitchen.

"Damn it." She rubbed the spot with the heel of her hand, hurrying onto the oven without slowing down. If that tray of artichoke dip didn't come out now, bad things were going to happen. Like the smoke alarm going off.

Shoving on an ancient hot mitt, tinted brown on the palm from years of abuse by screaming hot pans, she quickly pulled out the almost overdone appetizer and plunked it down on the stove, blowing a stray hair out of her eyes as she went. The smell of heavily browned, but not yet burnt cheese wafted up from the white baking dish. At least she'd missed that disaster. Even if only narrowly.

The clock on the back of the range clicked ahead another minute, driving home the fact she had ten minutes left to get it together before people started showing up.

Headlight beams flashed across the lace curtains covering the front windows.

"Shit." She dropped the mitt onto the glass cook top and tried to smooth back the wisps of hair escaping their tie as she rushed toward the front of the house.

Before she could reach it, the front door swung open, bringing in a swift shot of cold air and an unreasonable amount of relief as the first arrivals filed in.

"Oh thank God." If there was one thing her future daughter-in-law had it was great timing.

"What can I do?" Mina had her coat off and was in the kitchen washing her hands before Nancy could get the first word out.

Under normal circumstances she would have balked at the idea of a bride, especially this bride, helping with her own engagement party, but these were desperate times.

Nancy looked around the kitchen. It was clean at least, and the folding table intended to stand in as a pseudo buffet was set up under the far window and covered with a cloth, but that was as far as she'd gotten. "I need to start laying everything out. I don't even have the plates or napkins opened. I still need to get out all the chips and crack--"

"We got it. Don't worry." Mina peeked into the front room. "Kids, can you come in the kitchen?"

Within seconds, Mina's daughter and son, Maddie and Charlie were opening utensils and organizing them on the rectangular table. Mina pulled out serving bowls and filled them with chips and crackers and slider buns while Nancy arranged the appetizers and dropped in serving spoons. By the time people started walking through the door, the buffet was set perfectly and drinks were lined up across the counter.

Nancy wrapped her arms around Mina. "Thank you. You saved my ass."

Mina hugged her back tightly. "I've been told that I'm quite the ass-saver. You should have called me sooner." She pulled back and studied Nancy's face for a minute. "Or told us to throw our own damn party."

Nancy laughed shaking her head at one of her closest friends. "No way. I wanted to do it."

She needed something to celebrate. They all did.

Nancy swallowed the sudden sadness biting at the back of her throat and inwardly shook herself. She decided this morning that today would be happy and the only way to accomplish that was to push the still raw pain she felt about Rich to the back of her mind.

Tomorrow could be different. Tomorrow she could go back to missing him. To loving him because he was her son. And to hating him for what he'd done.

Unfortunately, that pretty much summed up the current state of her life. Stuck somewhere between love and hate, the guilt of both making it hard to accomplish much of anything.

"And we appreciate it." Mina smiled leaned back, giving her a once over. Her amber eyed gaze stalled on Nancy's chest. "I can handle down here while you go upstairs and put on a different top. That one is covered in...?" She raised an eyebrow in question.

"It's butter."

Mina grimaced. "I hope you don't like that shirt."

Nancy pulled it out and looked at the greasy streak running down the left boob of the pale pink blouse. She put it on earlier, hoping to save time, confident she could avoid making a mess of herself.

Another bad decision to add to a long list.

"Mina honey?"

Both women looked up at Thomas where he stood in the kitchen doorway, his still a little too lean frame propped against the jamb, leaning heavily on his good leg.

This time it was harder, with a grim reminder of the tragedies her family suffered staring her in the face, but come hell or high water, she was going to be happy tonight.

Plastering a smile on her face, Nancy shooed Mina in his direction. "Go greet your guests. I'll freshen up and be down in a minute." Thomas took Mina's hand in his and led her into the living room, now nearly full with guests, pride written all over his face. A tiny bit of the heaviness making her heart sag lifted.

The only way to get through this would be clinging to any little bit of good, any tiny scrap of joy she could get her hands on.

Taking advantage of the distraction Thomas and Mina brought, she ran upstairs to rectify the mess she'd made of herself. A fresh shirt, quick swipe with a hairbrush and a coat of tinted lip balm later she was back downstairs in the middle of friends and family.

Nancy managed a genuine smile and started across the room, greeting guests as she went. If it wasn't for the people around her, these past few months would have been even harder. They were nearly unbearable as it was.

She stopped to thank one of Thomas' classmates for sending food after Rich's funeral. Then, a frequent customer at the farmer's market who'd lost a child herself, squeezed her in a hug so tight she lost her breath. Another stopped her to ask about the antiques filling the house.

"I love this." The woman slid her hand along the side of the plain-lined walnut cabinet that took up a five foot section of the front wall between the door and window. "Where did you find it?"

Nancy couldn't help but touch the cabinet herself. The wood was smooth as glass under her palm. "The back forty. The tree it's made from fell in a storm and my dad had it milled and made this." It was as beautiful as it was treasured. Over the years its locked doors kept many a child from getting their little hands on a number of firing weapons. Until recently.

A movement at the back of the house, outside the kitchen windows, caught her eye. Speak of the devil.

She excused herself and made her way through the crowd.

The women of the room were oooo-ing and ahhh-ing over the stunning ring her son gave her friend, while the men were discussing whatever game had been on recently, making it easy to slip out unseen and head to the laundry room off the back of the kitchen.

Beth, Rich's widow, was just closing the back door as Nancy came around the corner, obviously surprising her, making the poor woman almost jump out of her skin. Beth's hand went over her heart as she let out a yelp and leaned back against the clothes dryer behind her.

"Oh!" She took a couple deep breaths and quickly regained her composure. "Hey. I'm sorry. We're a little late and I didn't want to disturb everyone."

"Nana!" Little arms grabbed Nancy around the waist and squeezed with all their might.

An easy smile of genuine joy spread over Nancy's face. "Hey girls." She dropped into a squat and wrapped her arms around Kate and little Liza. "I've missed you."

Kate giggled. "You just saw us yesterday."

"I know but I've missed you since then." She leaned in close to their little faces. "Maddie and Charlie are in the front room. I bet they've missed you too."

Both girls took off squealing, dropping their coats on the floor as they ran. Beth sighed as the girls disappeared into the crowd.

Nancy turned to her. "Hey." She hugged Beth tightly for as long as she dared, then did the next thing all mother's do when one of their own is suffering. "Are you hungry?"

She knew the answer. She'd been where Beth was, but had to try anyway. Even if only for herself. To feel like she was doing *something*.

"Not really." Beth grabbed the girls' coats off the linoleum floor and piled them on the dryer adding hers to the top. "Thanks though."

"I'm glad you came."

Beth leaned against the dryer. She looked tired. Her light brown was pulled back in a loose bun at the back of her head with a few fine strands turning into her face and tucking under her chin. The green of her eyes was still just as clear as ever, but her already fair skin looked pale and dull.

Beth chewed on her lip as she leaned forward to glance through the kitchen. "I wanted to." She blinked hard a few times in a row. "I don't want Mina to think I hate her or blame her for what happened."

Nancy wanted so much to hug her again. Squeeze her until the pain was gone, for both of them, but held back. Sometimes things like that only made it worse. No matter how well intentioned.

Instead, she smiled. "You're a strong woman."

Beth gave her a forced smile back. "It doesn't feel like it."

The voices in the house grew louder as the smell of food lured the hungry crowd to the kitchen. Beth peeked around Nancy and took another deep breath.

"It'll be okay honey."

Beth nodded quickly, her mouth set in a tight line. Her eyes caught Mina's where the other woman stood across the kitchen. Beth set her shoulders and headed straight for her.

The tiniest hint of envy bit at Nancy. If only she'd tackled things head on like that. Maybe her life would be different. Maybe all their lives would be different.

Nancy watched Mina's face as Beth headed toward her. The gentle smile she had when she first saw Beth quickly disappeared. Before Beth made it to her, Mina was shoving her cup and plate into Thomas' hands and stepping quickly to her.

The crowd edged out, giving the two women room as Mina put an arm around Beth and quickly led her to the front of the house, the sound of their feet on the stairs barely perceptible over the conversations filling the room.

Thomas crossed the kitchen toward his mother, winding his way through the bodies surrounding the buffet.

"What's going on?" His voice was full of concern.

"Probably the best thing that could happen for Beth right now. She's with one of the few people who can understand how she's feeling."

"Mina's having a hard time." He took a sip of his drink as his eyes moved across the faces filling the kitchen.

"I can imagine." Killing to save the man you love was one thing. Having to kill the cousin he considered a brother for the same reason, knowing you're taking a father from his children, a husband from his wife and a son from his mother? Very different. "Then maybe this will help her too."

They stood silently in the doorway, watching as their friends filled their plates, the sound of conversations filling the house. As the minutes ticked by Thomas became fidgety, shifting from foot to foot, checking his watch and craning his neck to try to see into the front of the house.

Nancy patted his back. "I'll go check on the girls."

She skirted the edge of the group and headed up the stairs, freezing at the second to last step. Through her closed bedroom door, she could hear Beth sobbing.

"I'm so sorry. I didn't know." Her words were choppy, broken apart by ragged breaths. "I never thought he would try to hurt someone."

Nancy moved to the door, her hand pausing at the knob. She held back.

Mina's voice was soft enough she could barely hear it through the heavy door. "Shhh. You could never have known what would happen. None of this is your fault."

Nancy's breath caught in her throat. She closed her eyes as she rested her head against the door.

"What will I tell my girls?"

Tears burned the back of Nancy's eyelids. The pain in Beth's voice cut like a knife reopening wounds from so long ago. It was a pain she knew. The worst she'd ever felt. A mother hurting for her children.

Nancy took her hand away from the doorknob and backed away. She wiped her eyes as she walked to the bathroom, silently closing the door behind her. Pulling a tissue free of the box she blew her nose.

Nancy allowed herself a few seconds to regroup, but that was all. This was supposed to be a party and she was being a terrible host. It was time to pop her head out of her ass and get it together. At least for a little bit.

She straightened her shoulders as she walked through the living room and into the kitchen. The first face she saw was her son's staring at her from across the room, still standing where she'd left him, but now he was surrounded by his buddies who were all laughing and joking.

Thomas was not.

Nancy made her way to him, greeting people as she went. The look on Thomas' face as he waited for her to reach him would have made her laugh if she wasn't still trying not to cry. She picked up the pace before he started to lose his mind.

"Everything's okay. Beth's just upset."

"With Mina?" His voice was loud. Louder than it should have been, making more than a couple of people turn their way.

"No honey. Beth isn't upset with Mina at all. If anything she's worried people are upset with her."

Thomas' jaw clenched and his eyes hardened. "She is just as much a victim as anyone else. Probably more."

He stood for a moment, his jaw so tight the muscles began to twitch. "I'm going up there."

Nancy grabbed his arm as he started to move. "No. Just give them a little bit."

Just then, Mina appeared at his side, a smile on her face that couldn't hide the sadness in her eyes. He pulled her against him and held her tight. "You okay?"

She leaned into his side and nodded her head. "Yeah."

"How's Beth?" His voice was low and soft.

"I told her we could keep the girls tonight and sent her home to take some time for herself." She leaned back, tipping her face to look up at him. "Is that okay?"

"Of course." He pecked her on the mouth. "Whatever you think will help."

Mina looked over the packed kitchen then at Nancy. "Sorry I disappeared. I saw her starting to cry and I didn't want her to feel embarrassed."

Nancy patted her arm. "Honey, you did the right thing." Just like always. Mina was the best person she'd ever known and adding her to their family was one more piece of happiness Nancy clung to.

Thomas' friend Jerry, a local cop, wandered over and started asking Mina about some home project he was planning and Nancy took the opportunity to slip away to check and see how the food was holding up to the hungry crowd.

She opened a couple more bags of chips and filled the waning bowls while chatting with people about her plans for the market this year, what new vendors had signed on, and when the best time to plant their peas would be.

The conversation helped take her mind off Beth and she started to relax a little, finally starting to enjoy the evening.

Nancy picked up a couple of empty dishes and headed to the sink, finding Mina was already there, lining up used serving spoons on the counter.

She set the dishes in the sink and turned on the faucet, hoping the hot water would soften the baked on crust left at the edges. "Are you guys ready for cake?"

She'd baked Thomas' favorite chocolate cake. Cakes. Three of them. That way he and the kids could take some leftovers home for later. Each was a triple layer, dark chocolate base with what amounted to a rich, fudgy, almost pudding like frosting. Just looking at it was enough to add ten pounds.

"We want cake! We want cake!" Kate and Liza came running, coming to a fast stop in front of Nancy.

"You girls have ears like bats." Nancy tousled Liza's hair before turning to get the cakes from the fridge.

"I want cake." Thomas stood right behind her a big grin on his face.

"Holy cow you're like vultures." She pointed at the refrigerator. "Pull one of them out and get it on the table. I'll grab a knife."

The first cake was demolished within five minutes. Nancy pulled out the second and set it on the table, leaving it for Mina to cut. She took away the serving disc from cake number one and chucked the silver coated piece of cardboard into the trash can. By the time she turned around, cake number two was halfway gone.

She should have made more cake.

Luckily, the sweet richness slowed the crowd down with only a few making it back for seconds. By the time the thinning crowd moved back into the living room, three-quarters of the third cake remained.

Nancy set the lid of a cake carrier over the surviving desert, protecting it from little fingers, and surveyed the kitchen. It looked like a tornado came through. She started collecting forgotten plates and misplaced cups but the sound of laughter in the front living room made her stop.

She dropped the trash in her hands onto an already full counter. It could wait. Soon her house would be empty and silent and she'd be wishing for someone to talk to. Might as well enjoy the company while she had it.

The kids sat on one side of the wide front room playing a board game they found in a large antique cupboard Nancy kept stocked with toys, books, movies and games. Now that she was spending more time with Beth's girls, it was coming in handy.

The adults congregated on the two large sofas and matching chairs, one of the few 'new' purchases Nancy made when filling her house. As beautiful as antique couches look, they are hell to sit on.

The group chatted casually about the long winter and Thomas and Mina's wedding plans until the kids started winding down. By the time the last guests were pulling out of the driveway little Liza was out cold, her chubby cheeks flushed from playing.

"Why don't you leave the girls with me?" Nancy tucked a blanket around the sleeping four year old. "She'll be out for the night and Kate and I can watch a movie."

Kate looked at Nancy, her eyes big. "Could I go home with them? Maddie said I could sleep in her bed."

Nancy couldn't blame her. Maddie did have the kind of bed most little girls dreamt of, especially the six-year-old variety. Paul built her a beautiful four poster bed with rails connecting the posts. Mina found lace panels to loop over the rails and wound twinkle lights all around the top. It really was beautiful. Even girls of the fifty-five-year old variety could appreciate it.

Nancy jumped up and ran to the kitchen. "I almost forgot." She quickly boxed up most of the remaining chocolate cake and headed back into the front living room, handing the container to Kate. "You can go with them as long as you promise not to eat all the cake for breakfast."

Kate clutched the cake to her chest, her face serious. "I promise."

Nancy collected their coats and helped get everyone loaded into Mina's van. By the time she made it back inside her teeth were chattering.

After locking the house up she scooped Liza off the couch and headed upstairs, ready to be cuddled up under the covers with her little snuggle bug.

She tucked the little girl in and quickly threw on her pajamas and brushed her teeth before scooting in beside her and leaning over to kiss her sweaty little head. As she looked into Liza's sweet face, Nancy wondered how long it would be before she'd be able to talk about her father without breaking down.

THREE

NANCY PARKED HER car facing the well-lit, downtown storefront. How did she let Mina talk her into this?

Dozens of people, all women, milled around the large room lined with long tables, stools and table-top easels. Nancy was many things but creative was not one of them.

A quick knock on the window beside her made her heart pound and stomach lurch. Autumn's smiling face was nearly pressed against the glass as she waved enthusiastically at Nancy. "Aren't you so excited?" Her voice was muffled by the glass but not her personality.

Autumn was married to Jerry, Thomas' lifelong friend. One of them anyway. She was as beautiful as she was animated. And bouncy. And happy. Hopefully her optimism about the evening was contagious.

Nancy shoved open the door and into a strong armed hug. "I'm so glad you came out with us." Autumn rocked their bodies back and forth as she squeezed. She pushed back but still didn't let go. "I haven't been out in so long I can't even remember. This is going to be the best night ever."

"Hey girls!"

Autumn's head craned to one side, her hands still firm where they held Nancy's shoulders. She let out a squeal and finally released Nancy to wave with her whole arm across the parking lot at Mina and Beth.

Within minutes Nancy was tied into a muslin apron, perched on a stool, sipping wine and staring down a blank canvas.

She leaned to her right. Mina was already swiping graceful streaks of a darkish green in purposeful strokes over her own canvas.

She peeked to the left. Autumn was squinting intently at her paintbrush as she mixed tiny dabs of paint together on her palette.

Even Beth was happily painting, a glass of white wine in one hand and a paint loaded brush in the other. She and Mina were chatting and giggling like old friends.

Nancy turned back to the glaringly white rectangle staring her down. She rolled up the sleeves of her sweater and grabbed

35

her brush. This couldn't be that hard. She'd painted before and done a decent job. Of course that was a barn.

Loading up, she slowly, carefully ran her brush in a horizontal line across the canvas exactly three-quarters of the way up.

There. Step one done.

She looked back up at the instructor who appeared to be at least on step four along with her friends. "Shit." She took a gulp of her wine and swiped on more paint before looking at the pictures in progress around her.

"Shit." She took another drink. She sucked at this.

"What's wrong?" Mina turned her way, her eyes getting wide when they landed on Nancy's masterpiece. "Oh."

Nancy grabbed her wine glass again. "I am awful at this."

Autumn leaned into her other side. "Holy cow you are." She giggled as she poured more wine into her own glass then filled Nancy's. "Drink more wine. You'll get better."

"Don't worry about it." Beth polished off her own glass and was reaching for the bottle herself. "You're just trying too hard."

"Isn't that what you're supposed to do?" Nancy stared at her own painting, but what was in front of her only earned the name in the literal sense. It was a collection of hard lined edges and exact proportions. "Maybe I'd be better at abstract."

"You'd be great at stripes." Ever the optimist, Autumn pointed at the perfectly straight lines of green, blue and orange. "They are perfectly symmetrical."

They all stared at what was supposed to be an evening sky as the sun met the ocean. Finally Mina spoke up.

"We should do something else for our next girl's night."

Nancy laughed. "Thank you. Maybe a cooking class. I can kick all your asses at that."

Everyone laughed with her. Beth hugged her from behind before taking her newly full glass of wine back to finish her own painting. Mina was still giggling as she went back to her beautifully blended painting, occasionally wiping at the corners of her eyes.

Autumn looked over from where she was fine-tuning an arching dolphin, jumping out of the water. "When do you think you'll open the market this year?"

She was one of Nancy's regular customers. A stay at home mom with four hungry boys trying their best to eat them out of house and home, her family went through copious amounts of produce.

Nancy tried to duplicate Autumn's perfect mammal, but it was looking more like a rock. She gave up and dropped her brush onto the tray in front of her.

"Probably early May. I won't have much until later in June though." Unless the weather kept taking its sweet time warming up. Then it would be mid-July before she had anything substantial.

"I can't wait. There's just nothing like home grown." Autumn's eyes were big and her smile even bigger. Exuberant was the perfect word to describe her. Nancy liked being around her. Her happiness was contagious. Nancy was feeling pretty darn good in spite of her terrible artistic skills.

Then again, maybe it was the alcohol.

"Why don't you start your own little garden?" Nancy blinked her eyes hard and poured herself some more wine.

Autumn's eyes got even wider as she shook her head. "Oh m'gosh. I wouldn't even know where to start."

Nancy swallowed the crisp white, for the first time trying to remember just how many glasses she'd had. "I can help you if you want."

"Really?" The pretty red-head nodded, her hair bouncing free from behind her ears. Autumn used both hands to tuck the strands on each side of her face back in place. "That would be so great. I could pay you for your help."

"Oh honey, no. I just want to help as a friend." With four boys and one salary that last thing that woman needed was to be paying someone to help her plant beans. "It would help me. Keep me occupied now that this one has my son to take care of." She grinned and thumbed over her shoulder at Mina. The tiny motion was enough to throw her a little off balance and she had to quickly grab the table to steady herself.

Mina started laughing behind her. "Nancy, your painting looks better than I remember." Beth was laughing and leaning into Mina's shoulder. "It certainly looks more presentable than Beth's."

Mina grabbed Beth's painting and held it up for the other two to see. She peeked over the top. "Her dolphin looks like a wiener."

Nancy cocked her head to one side, squinting at the gray shape. "Only if it's sad." She took a swallow of wine. "And uncircumcised."

The four women started cackling, loud enough that the rest of the class grew silent and turned their way looking more than a little aggravated.

Nancy bit her lip and looked straight ahead at her painting, trying to quickly finish up. The sound of occasional snickering came from both sides and frequently her. Luckily the class was nearly over and soon they were walking arm in arm into the parking lot. Mostly to hold each other up.

"We can't drive home." Mina giggled as she shoved Beth's painting on top of hers in the back of her minivan. "We'd end up in handcuffs before the night was over."

Autumn shrugged her shoulders. "When Jerry figures out I'm drunk I'll probably end up in handcuffs anyway."

"Ahhhhh!" The women fell against Mina's van laughing.

Nancy could hardly breathe and her stomach muscles hurt. Tonight was the most fun she'd had in... God, forever.

Eventually, they calmed down and Mina pushed off the van. "Seriously though. What are we going to do?"

Beth zipped her coat and pulled on her gloves. "I bet we can walk it off." She cinched her hood around her face.

Hiking around town at 10 at night didn't sound like fun, especially in the cold. Nancy shook her head. "Let's just call someone to come get us."

Beth slung her purse high on her shoulder. "Like who? You and I have no one to call and I'm pretty sure neither of these," she motioned at Autumn and Mina, "wants to confess their girl's night sins unless absolutely necessary."

The four looked at each other for a second.

"Let's go." Autumn tucked her hands in the pockets of her black parka and started walking with Mina hurrying to catch up, her path only slightly weaving.

"We can't just wander the streets." Nancy followed behind, trying to focus on each step to avoid stumbling. "Where in the world can we go?"

Mina stopped, nearly colliding with her. "I have an idea."

****

Paul slowed his truck peering across the dark lawn at the brightly lit house beyond it. He turned off the lights when he left. He was positive of it.

Cutting his head lights, he pulled into the empty driveway. If some son-of-a-bitch was there thinking they'd steal his tools... Let's just say they were about to have quite the surprise.

Moving carefully, he slid out of the truck and silently pushed the door closed, making a barely audible click. He crouched down and hurried over the lawn, the brown and slightly frozen grass crunching under the soles of his work boots, keeping his eyes glued to the uncovered windows of the house he and Mina were working on. If someone was in there, he had yet to see them.

Climbing the steps to the porch gave him a clear view into most of the house. The drywall was still not hung in this side of the building so he was able to scan quickly. No one. If someone was inside they were on the other side. The one he couldn't see without going in.

Muffled voices floated through the night air. Voices that were coming from inside the house.

His blood started to rush as his adrenaline spiked. No more sneaking. Someone was in there and he was about to make them fill their pants. With one swift kick from a heavy steel-toed boot, Paul knocked the door open and off one set of hinges.

He expected to be met with yelling and chaos, and he was, but of a completely different nature then he'd anticipated. He assumed the sight of him would send the men scrambling to get away. Instead he was met by screaming women. Running toward him. Armed with any sort of weapon they could grab.

His arms went up reflexively, shielding his head from the assailants.

"Paul?"

He peeked between his forearms, then dropped them altogether and straightened. These were women he knew well, all staring at him, weapons still clutched tightly in their hands.

Mina dropped the hammer she held cocked above her shoulder down to her side then looked toward the demolished front door, and back at him. "What in the hell are you doing?"

Beth propped against the flat shovel she'd grabbed and Autumn lowered her crowbar, their eyes wide and chests heaving. Autumn looked at Beth. "I knew I was right. This is the best girls night ever."

Beth started laughing, followed by Mina and Autumn.

What in the hell was going on here?

"You just kicked that door in." A fourth voice came from behind the other women.

Shit. No, no, no, no. Not her. Not here.

"Holy shit Nancy, did you see that?" Autumn pointed to the splintered wood trim hanging from the frame. "He just," the red head made a wide sweep with her arms, "boom!"

Four women ready to lynch him with his own tools was unsettling. Nancy seeing him make an ass out of himself was embarassing. But the fact she was holding his cordless drill, still fitted with a six inch bit was terrifying. So much so, he couldn't stop himself. He pointed at it.

"That's what you grabbed?"

Nancy looked down at the scuffed, well-used Craftsman in her hand then shrugged. "I grabbed what I thought could do the most damage and Beth already had the shovel."

At the mention, Beth lifted the thing and swung it through the air. "I was ready to defend myself."

"Me too." Autumn swung around the crowbar in a much less graceful movement. "We are bad-assed."

Paul rubbed his temples. "What are you even doing he--" He shook his head. "No. Never mind."

It was late. He'd worked all day, then taught a class and he just wanted to get out of here and away from these women, one in particular. "I'm going home." He pointed at the door. "I'll fix this in the morning."

"No, wait." Mina sidled up to him. "We need a favor." She looked around him and nodded her head. "We need you to take us home."

Paul paused. He looked at the woman beside him and realization dawned on him. Everything made a lot more sense. Now that Mina was close enough, he could smell the alcohol on her breath.

Autumn was at his other side. "We went to this painting place where you drink and paint and we mostly did the first part."

Beth was at Mina's side. "Can you take me home first? I have a sitter and she needs to be home by midnight."

They were everywhere. Their glassy eyes plastered to him as they pleaded their case. He was backed into a corner and they knew it.

"Fine."

Autumn bounced away. "Yay! I'll get my purse."

He stomped through the busted door and onto the empty porch. He inhaled, filling his lungs with the chilly early March air. How in the hell did he end up here?

A body bumped into him from behind. He looked over his shoulder to find Beth clutching the back of his coat, trying to regain her balance. She looked up at him, her green eyes wide.

"Sorry. I didn't realize there was a step there."

Mina came onto the porch next. She looked at his truck and groaned. "I forgot it was a two door."

The women filed down the steps and tugged open the passenger side door. "What is this big bag in the back seat?" Autumn tilted the front seat forward and leaned into the back. Her hand was wrapped around the handle just as Paul dropped his big mitt on the top of the bag.

"That stays there."

Mina looked in at him. "Can't it go in the back? We're going to be smoshed."

"Nope. It stays inside." Paul climbed in the driver's seat, refusing to elaborate any further. What he did in his spare time was no one's business but his.

His abrupt reaction didn't seem to faze Autumn at all. "That's okay. Beth and I will be just fine." She shoved Beth in first then climbed into the back behind her.

Mina suddenly started rummaging through her purse. "Crap. I left my keys inside. I'll be right back." She took off for the house leaving Nancy standing at the open door.

She shifted on her feet, looking more than a little uncomfortable.

The feeling was mutual. He didn't want to be here anymore than she did, but there was no way he was going to leave four drunk women to fend for themselves. Especially this group of women.

"Get in. It's freezing."

Nancy lurched forward as Mina shoved at her from behind. He'd been so busy trying to pretend she wasn't there he'd missed her almost daughter-in-law running down the driveway.

Nancy grabbed the dash, narrowly avoiding landing face first into his lap. The brain he'd been trying to convince of her non-existence grabbed onto the image and refused to let go. As she righted herself and slid across the seat his brain kept going, already off to a running start, imaging her sliding around and over him in much different ways. Better ways.

She tucked her arms tightly at her sides and carefully positioned herself so not even the smallest bit of their bodies touched.

"You're going to have to scooch more." Mina climbed in and undid all Nancy's careful placement, pushing her body tightly against his.

Her leg pressed warmly into his. Her side tucked neatly against him. The smell of wine and honey invaded him. Worst of all, the impact bounced her hand to his thigh. Just as the warmth of her palm seeped through his jeans, she yanked it away to grip the handle of her purse with white knuckles.

Mina kept shifting trying to get the volume of her overstuffed coat adjusted around her, making Nancy's body rub against his in a horribly unforgettable way.

He snuck a sidelong glance at the woman so close by his side. Her face was flushed red and her eyes were glued straight ahead.

Mina stared at him impatiently. "Paul. Let's go."

Shit.

He threw the truck in reverse and backed down the drive.

How long had he been staring? Did the women notice? Worse yet, did Nancy notice?

It was just another perfect example of why he tried to stay away from the woman. He didn't know how to act around her. Never did. That's probably why things went the way they did.

"You can stop right here." Autumn piped up from the back seat.

"Why?" He slowed the truck.

She pointed a finger out the windshield at a large brick two-story. "'Cause that's my house."

He put the truck back in park less than two minutes after leaving the house and turned to look into the back. "You live a block away?"

Autumn nodded.

Women made no sense. "Why didn't you just walk home?"

Autumn smiled broadly. "Because I was having the best night ever."

At least someone was.

FOUR

"IN THROUGH THE nose. Out through the mouth."

Nancy opened one eye and looked around. The rest of the room was peacefully face down, ass up. It was a position she hadn't been in in years.

Lots of years.

"Raise up, keeping the arms and the chest high, continuing to breathe deeply."

The man directing the class was keeping his voice low and soft. Nancy assumed it was supposed to be soothing and calming, but this whole situation was having the complete opposite effect on her. She was going crazy just sitting here. Breathing.

"You're not relaxing." Beth whispered in her direction, her own eyes still closed.

Nancy tried to lean back into the next pose with the rest of the class but kept losing her balance. "You don't know that."

Beth opened one eye. "I can feel it."

"I can't help it." Closing her eyes and looking inward was the last thing she wanted to do. "I'm trying but I don't think I'm cut out for relaxing."

"That is because you have not found your center." A deep male voice spoke so close to her ear she could feel his breath move across her skin, making her shiver. She immediately looked down.

Damn Mina.

The skin tight active-wear tank Mina loaned her for this class did nothing to hide the puckering of her nipples brought on by that damn shiver. Nancy tried to will away the reaction, but before she could make any headway, the yoga instructor spread his large, tanned hand over her stomach and pulled her back against his hard, naked chest.

"Here. This is where you breathe from. This is where you focus." He leaned down, his long dark hair tickling her bare shoulder as he slid both hands up her ribcage, high enough to tease at the underside of her breasts. "You are breathing from here. You must stop. You will hyperventilate."

Whether it was his hands on her, or his voice in her ear, Nancy had the sudden urge to start laughing. This was how her dry-spell would end? A strange, albeit devastatingly attractive, yoga instructor would be the first man to feel her up in so long she couldn't even remember? And of course it would be in front of a roomful of people.

Of course.

"Close your eyes."

She hated herself for it, but did as she was told. The feel of his large, solid body behind her, holding her, his deep voice in her ear, it was all a little overwhelming. Maybe closing her eyes was a good idea. Shut the big accent wielding yoga God out of her mind.

It worked.

Now, with her eyes closed, it wasn't Ricardo or whatever his name was behind her. It was Paul. Holding her, rocking her body back against his.

Her eyes flew open. "Nope." She squirmed away and scooted to the edge of the class grabbing her bag as she made a beeline for the exit.

"I'm so sorry." She backed toward the door. "I don't think this will help me at all."

Beth raised an eyebrow at her.

"I'm sorry." She mouthed the words and pushed the glass door open with her butt then all but ran to her car. Partly because it was freezing and she hadn't taken the time to put on her jacket, but mostly in an attempt to outrun the thoughts that just hijacked her brain.

Unfortunately, being the jerks they were, the damn things followed her as they had a habit of doing lately.

That was a lie. Not lately.

Always.

But now they'd changed. Maybe for better. Maybe for worse. All she knew was the once sweet imaginings she spent so many times lost in over the years were taking on a more salacious edge.

Nancy started the engine and cranked the heat before reaching into her bag to grab her jacket.

"Shit."

She let her head fall to the steering wheel and was still deliberating which fate was worse, freezing to death or going back inside, when the passenger door opened and her coat landed on her lap.

"What in the hell was that about?" Beth climbed in and pulled the door closed.

Nancy shoved one arm in and wrestled the rest of the garment across her back. "I'm sorry. You didn't have to leave."

"Um, yeah. I did. We rode together." Beth fished her cell out of her own bag. "Do you know how long I've been taking this class and never once has that man tried to feel me up. I kind of hate you right now."

She glanced up at Nancy, then down at her chest. "By the way, you're supposed to wear a sports bra with that."

Nancy looked down, then zipped her coat up to her chin. "It has a bra in it already."

"That's only good for controlling girls of the smaller variety if you know what I mean." Beth poked at the keyboard of her phone. "You've got the kind you need to double wrap." She dropped her phone in her bag. "Let's meet Mina and go shopping." She eyed Nancy. "Unless you plan on trying to abandon me at the mall too."

Nancy pulled out of the lot and toward the mall. "I wasn't trying to abandon you. It was just weird."

Bath raised her eyebrows. "Then I guess I'm in desperate need of some weird."

Nancy stared ahead, letting Beth's words marinate, mulling over the opportunity they just gave her and trying to decide if she should ask the question rolling around in her head. She swallowed. "How do you know you're ready to move on?"

She held her breath, not really sure how Beth would react to what could be considered a prying question, but it was also one she desperately wanted Beth to answer. Mostly because Nancy'd never been able to answer it for herself.

If she was being rude it didn't seem to faze Beth. The younger woman shrugged. "I don't know that I am, really." She looked at Nancy out of the corner of her eye as a small smile spread across her face. "But I like to think about it."

Huh.

Obviously Nancy didn't do so well with that either considering she just bolted from a yoga class at the thought of a man touching her.

Maybe all these years later, she still wasn't ready. Or maybe it was because the only man she'd ever wanted to move on with acted as if she was contagious. Or on fire. Or both.

She and Beth found Mina sitting on a bench, her phone against her ear, eyebrows drawn together. She rolled her eyes at her phone as she disconnected the call and shoved it into her purse. "That man."

"Thomas being difficult?" Nancy feigned shock. She, better than anyone else knew what a pain in the ass her son could be.

"Paul. He's still crabby with me about the other night." Mina stood up and pointed at a shop across the walkway. "I need to go there."

Nancy followed behind the younger women wondering why exactly Paul was so upset. Maybe because they nearly assaulted him. Maybe because he destroyed the front door because of them. The memory sent a thrill burning through her body until another, more likely option, occurred to her, effectively dousing the flames.

"Maybe we kept him from something. His girlfriend maybe." Nancy grabbed the closest thing on a hanger, already kicking herself. Paul's personal life shouldn't matter to her. He'd had years to make it matter to her. If he wanted it to, it would have happened by now.

And yet she was holding her breath waiting for Mina's reply.

Mina snorted. "Paul hasn't had a girlfriend in all the time I've known him." She rifled through a stack of high-cut cotton panties, collecting a few in one hand. "He could probably use a good--" Mina pointed at the garment still clutched in Nancy's hands. "That's really pretty. Are you going to get it?"

Nancy looked down at the nearly translucent, pale pink, lace bra she held. "Oh." She quickly hung it back on the rack. "No. I would never wear something like that."

Beth grabbed it and shoved it back at her, then started adding more. "That's the saddest thing I've ever heard."

Nancy struggled to keep hold of all the items as Mina joined in. Matching bra and panty sets, most of which didn't have enough fabric to cover one boob, let alone two. "Why in the world would I wear any of these?"

Beth grabbed her arm and led her to the dressing rooms at the back of the store. "For you." Beth shoved her into an empty stall. "We've sucked at finding you a hobby, but we can absolutely make sure you feel sexy." She pulled the door shut. "Try them on. Trust us."

Nancy held up the scant scraps of fabric. Never in her life had she worn anything like this. But never in her life had she felt sexy either. Pretty, yes, sexy...

"Are you in one?" Mina's voice on the other side of the door made her jump.

"I'm going." She looped the hangers over the hook and twisted her way out of Mina's magenta tank. The thing might as well have been made out of rubber bands. It would have been easier to wrestle off.

She grabbed the bra at the front. The same pink, lace, wisp of a thing she'd accidentally grabbed when they first came in. When she was distracted, thinking about Paul.

Nancy fingered the delicate fabric wondering what a man would think of something like this. What Paul would think of something like this. Not that it mattered. The chances of him, or any man for that matter, seeing it were slim to none based on her track record.

It would be her little secret.

Nancy slid the straps over and up her arms, hooking the loops at her back. She pushed the fullness of her breasts fully into the cups and stared at her reflection, more than a little surprised by what she saw.

Maybe she hadn't been giving sexy enough credit all these years.

****

"Like this?" Charlie carefully held the drill perpendicular to the plywood and turned to Paul for approval.

He nodded. "Perfect. Start slow in case it tries to jump around."

Charlie gently pulled the trigger and the bit began to twirl, eating into the wood.

"Good job. Keep going. Remember it will drop quick when you get all the way through so don't lose your grip." Paul resisted the urge to step closer. He was simply here as a skilled assistant.

The drill poked through the back side but Charlie barely let it drop. Paul grinned, proud at how well the kid was doing. "Now keep it moving while you pull it back up."

Mina's son did as he was told, brushing away the tiny shavings left behind to inspect his work. "I did it." He looked up as Mina came into the garage. "Mom look, I drilled the hole for the wheel mounts."

Mina looked over his shoulder. "Buddy that looks great." She picked up the plans for the gravity racer they were in the process of building. Her brow furrowed. "There's no front end on this."

"Paul said you would say that." Charlie handed her the updated version they worked out. "That's what ours will look like."

She was as predictable as she accused him of being. Paul knew Charlie would never get the chance to sit in the original design, let alone race it. "We worked out a front end that would protect him just in case."

Mina looked up at him and he gave her a wink. "We can even line the thing in pillows if you want."

She walked past him and slapped the papers into his chest. "Don't act like you wouldn't have done it anyway."

She was right. He'd never let Charlie race an open-front boxcar either, but he'd never admit to it now.

"Dinner's almost done boys." She pointed at Paul. "I made your favorite dessert as a thank you for helping."

"You don't have to thank me." He tipped his head in Charlie's direction. "This guy's doing most of the work."

Mina opened the door to go inside. "So you don't want to stay for dinner?"

"I wouldn't go that far." If it kept him from another night of cold bologna on bread, he'd help Charlie build a whole fleet of those racers.

Paul turned to Charlie. "Let's clean up. I'm hungry."

They were finished and inside washing their hands when the doorbell rang. "You expecting someone?"

Charlie twisted his hands in the towel above the toilet and shrugged. "It's probably Nana. She comes over a lot." The boy took off in a hurry, leaving Paul alone in the downstairs half bath.

He considered staying there.

His reflection stared back at him as he scrubbed any hint of dirt from under his nails and around his cuticles. The hair on his face didn't quite classify as a beard, just laziness. The hair on his head could be explained the same way. If that was Nancy out there, she wouldn't be impressed.

Not that it mattered. She was out of his league. Always had been. Always would be.

Not that he hadn't tried anyway when he was young and ballsy. He'd come in second. Not quite enough of what she wanted to make her chose him.

Story of his life.

He dried his hands then ran them through his hair without thinking, smoothing it into a less unruly pile of salt and pepper waves.

Damn. Even after all this time, his subconscious still held out, torturing him, reminding him of her and what might have been.

He grabbed the door handle. Might as well get this over with. Might not even be her.

He could only hope.

Yanking the handle, he pulled the door open quickly, mostly to prove to himself he wasn't a coward. If it was her, he'd handle it like a man. He'd—

"Oh shit." A body tumbled in through the door.

Nancy stared up at him, her chin planted in the middle of his chest, her hands twisted in his shirt.

He held perfectly still, partly from shock and partly because he didn't want her to fall on the ground. "Are you okay?"

She blinked and looked side to side as her cheeks began to flush. "I think so."

At least he wasn't a total idiot and did manage to grab her as she fell against him. He tried to use his grip to help her get back on her feet and out of his arms. He moved slightly and her breath caught.

"Are you hurt?" She hadn't seemed to hit anything besides him as she fell.

Her eyes darkened and she quickly licked her lips as she shook her head.

He felt her shiver against him. It was no wonder. She was wearing some sort of sleeveless shirt. It felt thin under his palm. Hell, he could feel the tightness of her nipple through the damn thing.

Oh, God.

He swallowed hard as she continued to watch him, making no move to step out of his arms. Or from under his hand.

But then again he wasn't moving either.

"Dinner!" The sound of Thomas' voice down the stairs was enough to snap Nancy into action.

She jumped back two feet and her gaze dropped to the floor. "I just needed to wash my hands."

He cleared his throat and stepped past her. "I'll leave you to it then."

REGRET

The door clicked shut behind him as he all but ran up the stairs to the dining room, trying to put as much distance between him and Nancy in that damn skin tight outfit she had on.

His escape was only temporary. Very temporary, because as soon as Nancy appeared upstairs, her face still flushed from their run-in, she was quickly ushered by Mina's daughter directly toward him.

"Are you sure you have enough? I really don't need to stay." Nancy stood behind the seat next to him. The seat Maddie requested she sit in.

Mina cocked her head to one side. "Of course I have enough. Sit down and stop being considerate."

Nancy pulled the chair out and slid in, not even coming close to him as she went. Probably on purpose and it was much appreciated on his end. Almost as much as the sweatshirt she'd borrowed from Mina.

At least now he couldn't see the full breast that just a few minutes ago filled his right hand. Couldn't see it, but hell if he could still feel it. The warmth. The softness. The tight bud of her nipple pressed against the lifeline crossing the center of his palm.

"How was yoga?" Thomas held a forkful of macaroni and cheese in front of his mouth as he watched Nancy, waiting for her reply.

Nancy rolled her eyes and stabbed at the food on her plate. "Let's just say I don't think I'll be going back any time soon."

Mina snorted across the table. "The instructor got a little handsy."

Thomas lifted an eyebrow and Nancy buried her head in her hands.

Charlie looked around the table, his brow wrinkled in confusion. "What's handsy mean?"

Maddie piped up, all too eager to share her teenage wisdom. "It's when a guy tries to feel a girl's bo--"

"Maddie!" Mina's voice was almost as sharp as the glare she leveled at her firstborn.

Paul wanted to die.

No. That was an exaggeration. But he absolutely wanted to get the hell out of here. Far, far away from this conversation. Far away from her.

Of all the nights to help Charlie, he had to choose this one.

The table stayed silent until Thomas finally shook his head and chuckled. "Well, I guess I can see how that would make things weird."

FIVE

NANCY GRABBED HER favorite lined, canvas work shirt from the hook where it dangled by the back door and pulled it on over her sweater, stabbing each button through its corresponding hole.

She walked out the back door and onto the deck. A cold, strong, wind whipped at her hair, making her glad she'd added the extra layer. It was spring for Christ's sake. The weather needed to catch up. This gloom and cold was wearing on her. It wasn't the only thing.

Hopefully some physical labor would help get her head on straight.

Nancy huffed as she trudged down the steps to retrieve the wheelbarrow from behind the shed at the back corner of her lot.

The steamy air curling from her breath was a warning that it was colder than it seemed, and it seemed pretty cold.

After less than fifteen minutes of ripping out dried up stalks of formerly lush, green, tomato plants from the soggy ground, the cold dampness of the dirt and the day was seeping into her work gloves, the chill making her fingers ache all the way to the bone. She probably had freaking arthritis. Lovely.

A sudden gust of wind grabbed the stalk she'd just stuffed onto the top of her wheelbarrow and whipped it away, dropping it twenty feet across the yard, where it was going to have to stay. Today wasn't the kind of day to spend trying to clear out the crap from last year's garden, but sitting in that house was making her crazy.

Then she would be arthritic and insane. Unfortunately, after last night the latter felt pretty damn accurate.

That was the reason she was out here suffering in the first place. Trying to wrap her brain around what happened in Thomas and Mina's bathroom.

She was at a point where she was finally beginning to accept her current relationship with Paul was all it would ever be. After thirty years, it was time to call it what it was.

Nothing. The man simply didn't want her like she wanted him.

Not that she blamed him. After what she'd done to him it was a miracle he would even look at her. It was a tough pill to swallow, but she almost had it down.

Then last night happened.

Last night he'd done more than look at her. Much more.

It was an accident, she knew that. He didn't intend for her boob to land in his hand. But it wasn't so much what happened that she was focused on. It was what didn't happen that was causing this inner turmoil.

Most people, men included, would immediately yank their hand away when they realized it was in a compromising location. Paul didn't. Even after it was clear he knew exactly what he held. He didn't pull his hand away. Quite the opposite.

He'd caressed her.

That alone would have been enough to confuse the hell out of her. But there was more.

Nancy could swear, from her position pressed tightly against his chest, she heard the faintest of sounds rumble through his chest.

A growl.

She'd been out of the game for a long time, but Nancy knew one thing for sure.

Uninterested men didn't growl.

Pulling off her gloves, she pinched them between her thighs as she tugged the elastic around her pony tail free then tried to recapture the wayward strands with stiff fingers. By the time the gloves were back on, the shorter strands around her face began to work free again, curling up her nose and into her eyes.

"Damn wind." She grabbed the handles of the wheelbarrow and started rolling it across the loose dirt. This was a losing battle and it was only making her more frustrated.

The wheelbarrow bumped along as she directed around the shed to one of the composting piles to dump the little bit of dried vegetation that made it into the bucket.

For a second she considered grabbing a shovel to turn the heaps of kitchen scraps and yard waste over, but a whip of wind made her rethink. The way her life was going she'd end up with a face full of compost bits to pick out of her teeth.

After tipping the wheelbarrow bucket side down and tossing her gloves in the shed, she locked it up and stomped her way back across the deck. Once in the house, she chucked her mucks on the mat just inside the back door. Her numb fingers fumbled with the buttons of her shirt until she gave up and went to the living room to flop on the couch and wait for the warmth inside to bring the feeling back.

Nancy crossed her arms and shoved her hands up into her armpits, hoping the added heat would speed up the process. She looked around the house and waited, trying to think of something besides the tiny idea growing in the back of her brain.

The ache in her fingers was finally beginning to subside so she had another go at the buttons on her coat. This one was successful. She slipped her arms out and went to the back door, hanging the coat back on its hook.

While she was there, Nancy opened the dryer door to see if by chance it contained a forgotten load of laundry that could be fluffed and folded. It was empty.

She wandered into the kitchen and double checked the sink for dishes. Also empty. There wasn't a crumb on the floor. No smear of food on the counter either. Nothing to fold, nothing to sweep, nothing to wipe.

Oh my God, why couldn't she have found a hobby? Something to occupy her time other than remembering Paul's body pressed against hers. His hand cupped over her breast, the thinnest of fabric separating his flesh from hers.

She shivered again, but this time it was not because she was cold.

It was so confusing. He was so confusing.

When he thought Mina and her kids were in danger, Paul was right beside her, making sure everyone was okay, helping Nancy get them through.

Then he fell off the face of the Earth.

One minute he was buying her wiper blades and putting them on her car. The next he was gruffly refusing to come to her party and walking away.

Now he'd had his arms around her and his hand on her breast. Who knew what he would do after that. Probably join the Peace Corps so he could go to another continent.

The man wasn't just confusing. He was frustrating as hell.

The tiny idea she tried to ignore bloomed.

Nancy stood up and stomped to the hook where she'd just replaced her work coat. She shoved her arms in and buttoned up. This was ridiculous.

There was only one way to find out what was going on in that brain of his. It wasn't going to make Paul happy, but she didn't seem to be too good at that anyway.

One way or another she was going to figure him out. Figure out where she stood. Where they stood. Until then, he was going to have to get used to being around her.

Luckily, she had a perfect excuse.

****

Paul popped his knee into the line he scored across the sheet of drywall next in line to be hung, then ran his blade along the resulting crease on the back side, separating the piece he needed. "You done there little girl?"

Mina leaned into the drywall screw gun, sinking the last screw into the seam. "I think so."

She hooked the gun on her waistband and helped him get the newly cut section into position. They were three-quarters done with the largest bedroom in the house. After this, it was on to common areas. If they hit it hard for a couple days, they should be ready to mud by the weekend.

Mina started screwing as he held the gypsum in place. She was uncharacteristically quiet today and that could only mean one thing.

"Can I ask you a question?"

Shit. He was about to fake a heart attack when he was saved by the sound of the door opening. He almost grinned at the perfect timing of the building inspector. If he hadn't quit drinking, he'd buy the guy a beer.

Only it wasn't the building inspector.

"You guys need a hand?" Nancy stood in the doorway smiling, one eyebrow cocked.

Mina looked at Nancy, then at him, then back at Nancy. "Um."

Any other time the girl has no shortage of words to yammer on with, but the best Mina can come up with now is 'um'? He looked sideways at her, willing her to say something, anything cause he sure as hell wasn't going to be encouraging Nancy to stay.

As luck would have it, Mina couldn't either. There was nothing for Nancy to do. Not until it came time to paint and clean, but he'd cross that bridge when he came to it. Until then he would happily go another day without Nancy Richards invading his life.

Nancy pointed at the screw gun in Mina's hand. "Do you have another of those? I know how to hang drywall."

Shit. Of course she did.

Mina shook her head. "I only have this one here."

Nancy stepped further into the room, close enough that he could see the pink on her cheeks and smell the crisp outside air she brought in with her. Her eyes lingered in his direction.

"Is there something else I could do to help?" Her voice was soft and only occasionally aimed at Mina. Just like her eyes, most of her words seemed to be directed at him.

"Um." Mina climbed down the ladder and looked around.

REGRET

A cell started to chime.

"Sorry." Mina slid her phone from her back pocket and answered.

"Oh no." Mina shoved the screw gun in Nancy's direction. "Okay. I'll be there in five minutes. I'm just down the street."

Mina slid her phone back in her pocket. "I have to go. Charlie is sick."

Paul breathed a sigh of relief. "We can quit for the day then." He started to untie his tool belt.

"I'll help you finish. That way Mina will have one less thing to worry about." Nancy looked around the room. "You're almost done here anyway. It would be silly to stop now." She stepped closer and started unbuttoning her coat, the movement pushing an exotic scent into the air around them. "And I'd hate to come all this way for nothing."

Keeping his eyes from watching her hands as they moved down, working each button slowly lose from its noose, was nearly impossible. It was a scenario he'd imagined many times over the years, Nancy teasing him, slowly unbuttoning her blouse as he watched, his pulse spiking, breath choppy, as he waited for that first glorious glimpse of her—

"Are you sure you don't mind?" Mina's voice jolted him back into reality. Terrifying reality.

Nancy smiled at him. "Not at all." She finally turned to Mina, giving him the chance to breathe. A reprieve from the torturous closeness of her body.

"Let me know how he is and don't worry about this." She motioned to the room around them. "We'll get it all finished."

Then Mina was gone, leaving him alone with Nancy. She turned to him and hooked the screw gun onto her waistband. Without another word she was up the ladder, picking up where Mina left off.

She was quick and precise, moving up and down the ladder without hesitation, never missing a stud and sinking each screw head. Nancy was a hell of a good drywall hanger.

It was one more terrible thing to add to the list. All he wanted was one flaw to cling to. One negative characteristic he could repeat like a mantra. A forget Nancy Richard's chant. She wasn't making it easy for him.

The woman was perfect. Horribly fucking perfect.

She stood back and looked around the room. "Is that it?"

"Yeah. Thanks." He unhooked his tool belt and went straight to the front of the house. It was time for her to go home. To get as far away from him as possible, as fast as possible. He opened the front door and turned to her. "Have a good night."

She stayed where she was on the other side of the living room, staring at him.

"You should go. Check on Charlie." Maybe reminding her of her sick grandson would be enough to get her feet moving.

He needed her to go now before he forgot himself. He knew all too well what being around her resulted in.

Wanting to be around her more. Hoping for things that weren't meant to be his. Not before. Not now. Not ever.

Paul grabbed his shirt off the folding chair by the door and shoved his arms in the sleeves. If she wasn't going, he was.

"Paul, I'm sorry." Her whispered words stopped him in his tracks. "So, so sorry."

Her eyes glistened in the faint light coming from the kitchen beside her. She stepped closer to him. Close enough he could smell the perfume that teased his nose before. It was so different from what he would expect her to wear.

In all his thoughts of her, she smelled sweet. Like sugar, maybe vanilla. Not this deep, rich scent invading the deepest parts of his brain. It was sensual. It was mysterious. And he would never forget it as long as he lived.

He cleared his throat. "You don't have anything to be sorry for."

She nodded. "I do. Unfortunately many things."

Her eyelashes fluttered quickly and her throat rippled as she swallowed hard. "I knew Sam was your friend. I shouldn't have-_"

He shook his head. "That was over thirty years ago. It's okay. I promise."

She stepped closer leaving little more than a paper's width between them. She barely had to tip her head back to look at him. "You're the only man who's never lied to me. Please don't start now."

He held perfectly still, hoping if he tried hard enough, she wouldn't see right through him. "I don't know what you want me to say."

"I want you to say I didn't ruin your life too." A tear slid down her cheek as she pressed her lips tightly together. "I've made so many mistakes in my life Paul. Walking away from you is the one I regret the most." Her breath hitched in her throat.

He wanted to wrap her in his arms, hold her body against his like he dreamed of doing so many times. He couldn't. He didn't trust himself. She needed comfort and he didn't know that would be the reason he was holding her.

"Everything's okay. I'm fine." He crossed his arms, tucking his hands tightly under his biceps keeping them where they belonged.

Nancy nodded.

"Okay." She took a deep breath and straightened her shoulders. "Then I guess I should go."

She looked into his eyes for a few seconds more. He held his breath and tried to be stoic. She wanted him to ask her to stay and hell if he didn't want the same damn thing. But he couldn't. He could never be what she needed. What she deserved.

She might regret it, but Nancy had it right the first time.

Nancy leaned in, his folded arms between them, and pressed a soft kiss against his cheek. If he hadn't been too lazy to shave, he would have felt the softness of her lips against his skin. Instead, he had to settle for the slight puff of her breath through his three-week beard.

"Goodbye Paul."

She turned and left.

Watching through the front door, he rubbed his cheek as she walked to her car and backed down the driveway. He had a sinking feeling Nancy Richards just walked away from him for the second time, only this time it wasn't because of his best friend.

This time, it might be because of him.

SIX

"IT'S BEAUTIFUL HERE." Nancy kept pace with Thomas as they rounded a curve in the trail, the dirt path obscured by last November's fallen leaves, compressed together by the heavy snow that only recently melted.

"It's way better than gimping along on a treadmill I can tell you that." Thomas kept a smooth rhythm with his gait even though he still needed a walking stick for balance and extra support. He moved the stick ahead, followed swiftly by one foot, then the other.

"I can't believe how much strength you've regained." Nancy stayed close beside him just in case. Hiking might be more fun than a treadmill, but it was also more dangerous. Especially here. The trails wound around hillsides resulting in beautiful views but also the occasional steep drop biting at the edge of the path.

Thomas lost a significant amount of tissue in his thigh. Nobody knew just how much he would be able to compensate for the injury. They still didn't know. As long as each day was better than the one before, that was all she could ask for. But facts were still facts. Thomas wasn't the man he was last season and might not be ever again.

"Do you think you can handle the fields alone this year?" Nancy hated to ask the question. It was a touchy subject, but one that had to be addressed. The spring planting was approaching quickly.

Thomas wanted to believe he was 100 percent, but the truth was, he wasn't. Not yet anyway, and the added physical stress and manual labor required might set him back further.

"Mina says I need to call the high school. See if there are any kids interested in summer work."

Nancy almost laughed. She thought she'd be starting a fight by simply suggesting he might not be capable. She should have known Mina would already be looking out for her son. That girl always was.

"That's a great idea."

Thomas slowed down a tiny bit. "I hate it anyway."

Nancy pretended not to notice his movements were becoming less smooth and he was leaning more heavily on his cane. "I know." She shrugged. "Maybe by next year."

Thomas shook his head. "I don't think so."

Nancy's heart twisted. Knowing it and hearing it from him were two different things.

He poked her with his elbow. "It's okay. We'll just have to figure out a more permanent option."

Nancy nodded. "Speaking of." She hesitated, not wanting to dredge any deeper than they already had, but like it or not, decisions had to be made. "What are we going to do about the books?"

The canopy covering the trail opened up into an open field. It was still brown and dry, and the tree line edging the flat expanse was a bramble of bare branches and fallen vines, but the tiniest hint of spring color peeked from under the brush. But with the sun shining down and a slight breeze swaying the wheat colored grass, it was beautiful.

Thomas eased onto a bench set at the side of the trail. It continued on, but it wasn't hard to imagine most people stopped right here. The serenity and peace of the spot was difficult to ignore.

He propped his cane between his knees. "I've been looking over what we found in Rich's office and it looks like he did a decent job of keeping things organized. It doesn't appear too overly difficult so I think Mina and I should be able to handle them."

That didn't surprise her. Thomas was always the kind of man who handled things himself. Even at his own expense. Not that Mina was any better. "I just don't know honey." Nancy chose her words carefully. "It's a lot of work and Mina already has so much on her plate."

Thomas shrugged. "I don't see any other way. I think we can work on it together at night and at least get through this year while we try to figure something else out."

Nancy wasn't backing down. "You have kids now. Don't forget that. They need a family."

Thomas leaned back, tipping his head and closing his eyes against the sun. "I know. I just don't know what else we're going to do." He took a deep breath before sitting back straight. "Bringing someone in at this point would almost be as much work just trying to train them. Not to mention there's nothing to pay them with until the end of the season."

The tightness of his voice mirrored the tightness in her heart. Nancy stared across the field trying to regain some of the peace she felt earlier. "There's that too."

She'd raised a man who stole from his family. Bled the business dry trying to save himself.

They sat quietly for a minute. Nancy struggled to come up with another option. Any other option.

"What about Beth?"

Thomas looked at her. "You think she could?"

Nancy sat up straighter. Beth was off in the summers. "I know she could, but..."

Thomas finished her thought. "She has so much to worry about right now."

"Yes she does and I wanted to talk to you about that." Nancy'd been thinking about Beth's financial situation, trying to come up with a way to help get her feet back under her. "Beth only has about six more months in the house."

"If she can make it that long." Thomas crossed his arms, his jaw set. So far he'd seemed to struggle the most with what Rich did to his own family. To him it was one thing to try to hurt a grown man, but another for Rich to do what he'd done to his family, particularly Beth, a woman he was supposed to care for and protect.

"How long does Mina think it will take to finish your house?"

He looked up, an odd look crossing his face. Maybe he thought it was a bad idea.

"Paul would be the one to ask about that. He's dealt with more new construction than she has." He pulled his phone from his pocket.

Of course he would be the one to ask. She was hoping for a day without any sort of Paul. To temporarily act as if he didn't exist. Because as confused as she felt about him yesterday, she was twice as perplexed today.

Going to help with the house Mina was working on was supposed to be the start of figuring out where she stood with Paul. The first step in putting that part of her life to bed. Maybe even moving on. Unfortunately, for some reason she struggled with that. Especially when it came to Paul. Because the truth was, she didn't want to move on from him.

She wanted to move on *with* him and it made her do all sorts of stupid things. Like wear new perfume and initiate awkward conversations.

She tried not to listen as Thomas began his conversation, but the pull was too strong. Part of her desperately wanted to hear what Paul would say to her son.

Who was she kidding? All of her wanted it.

"Hey angel. How's your day going?"

Her disappointment was laughable. Hell most everything she did lately was laughable.

"Really?" Thomas took a quick glance her way out of the side of his eye.

Mina's voice didn't carry across the outside air, leaving Nancy to hold her breath wondering what was being said.

"Yup. Love you too." Thomas hung up the phone and held it in his lap.

That was a short conversation and none of it included when his house would be ready. Nancy's stomach twisted nervously. Maybe Paul said something. Maybe Mina was upset with her for showing up unannounced yesterday. She did seem a little odd before she left.

Thomas stretched his injured leg out, pointing his toe toward the sky. "I figured Paul was with her, but I guess he stayed home today."

Nancy tried not to panic. No way would he quit working with Mina because of her. Paul was not that kind of man. If he said he would do something, he did. And he told Mina he would help her with Thomas' house. "Is he sick?"

Thomas' tapped his other boot on the matted grass under their feet as he flipped his cell over and over in his hands. Finally he looked up at her.

"What happened with you and Paul?"

She was right. Mina was weird yesterday. Come to think of it, her future daughter-in-law was a little strange the night before at dinner too. All this time she was focused on Paul and how he was acting. It never occurred to her to pay attention to how *she* was acting.

It was probably obvious as hell.

Nancy scratched at a nonexistent spot on her jeans as she worked through an answer.

Thomas sighed beside her. "I'm just asking because Mina's going to start driving me nuts if I don't have an answer soon." He turned to her. "And then she's going to start asking Paul."

Part of Nancy wanted to hear how Paul would explain what went on between them. It was only a little part though. The rest of her was terrified of what he would say. And what it would make Mina think of her.

"We knew each other in high school." Nancy closed her eyes and took a deep breath of the barely warm air and mulled over how to explain their history. Her history. "More than knew each other I guess. I liked him, I knew he liked me."

"Before dad?"

She nodded, trying to swallow the lump forming in the back of her throat. "Right before your dad." Her voice was barely a whisper.

She cleared her throat. "They were friends." She shook her head, ashamed to admit the truth. Even worse, for her son to know it. "Best friends."

Thomas stayed quiet, waiting.

"Paul and I went out on one date. He was the nicest guy." She remembered it like it just happened, sometimes it felt like it just did. Maybe because she'd replayed it so many times over the years. It was one of the best nights she'd ever had, but at the time, she didn't appreciate it.

Paul was quiet and kind and a perfect gentleman. Traits a seventeen-year-old girl wouldn't value until years later. He'd taken her to a movie and dinner in the beautiful car he'd worked his ass off to pay for. A bright orange GTO.

Then, she'd fucked it all up.

"Your dad asked me out the next day."

Thomas' eyebrows went up. "Wow." He shook his head. "Dad just fucked everyone didn't he?"

Nancy sighed. As much as she wished she could blame it all on Sam, that wouldn't be fair. "It wasn't just your dad's fault."

Thomas studied her for a second. "Why'd you pick him?"

It was something she'd struggled with for years. The truth was stupidity. Arrogance. "I was a dumb, superficial girl." And she suffered greatly because of it. Lots of people had. "Your dad was the captain of the football team. The homecoming king. I suppose I was just captivated with the fact he wanted me."

"Why didn't you guys try again after dad? I mean, you were both single."

"He never asked again." She always hoped, maybe one day he would, but anytime they ran into each other it was obvious he wasn't thinking the same thing. Not until a few months ago when he helped her with Maddie and Charlie. Then she thought there might be a chance he wanted to see what could happen between them.

But he didn't. She didn't hear from him again.

"Have you talked to him about what happened?" Thomas' tone was gentle, but she knew he didn't blame Paul. She couldn't either.

"Last night."

Thomas cocked his head to the side. "Last night?"

"Yes." Nancy rubbed her temples.

Thomas reached across to put his hand on her arm. "He might just need a day to himself. Don't worry."

Nancy swallowed. "He's such a good man. He didn't deserve what I did." She held her breath and clamped her hand over her mouth as an unexpected flood of emotion threatened to overwhelm her.

After a few seconds, when she felt confident the chances of her either breaking into sobs or screaming like a lunatic were significantly reduced, Nancy dropped her hand. "I don't know how to fix it. I just wanted him to know how sorry I am."

Sorry for him, sorry for her, sorry for Thomas, and sorry for Rich. When she chose Sam over Paul, she sealed all their fates. Even Beth and the girls were suffering because of her and the guilt was eating her alive.

Maybe Paul wasn't the only one she owed an apology.

"I'm sorry to you too."

Thomas scoffed. "You weren't the problem."

"Well, I chose the problem didn't I?" Nancy rubbed her hands over her face. Her head was beginning to hurt. "Let's talk about something else. I can't..."

"We need to get Beth and the girls taken care of." Thomas turned his outstretched leg slowly from side to side. "I don't know that Mina and I decided where we were going to live. I think with everything going on, we figured we would decide later."

Which house they wanted was the least of her worries. "Can we swing all the houses?"

"If Beth can help with the books it would be no problem." He paused while he stood from the bench. "I'll go home and run the numbers. The hardest part will be now until the fall when our money comes in, but we should be able to get through."

Thankfully Thomas took his entire share each year at the end of the season. Over the years Rich tried many times to get him to keep it in the pot and take an allowance, promising he could invest it and make Thomas even more money. He'd never taken him up on the offer thank goodness, opting for the certainty of money in the bank instead. If he had, they would be really screwed right now.

"Do you think Mina will mind?" It was a lot to ask of her. She would basically be helping support Beth.

Thomas shook his head. "Mina's been asking some questions that in hindsight make me wonder if she was already thinking this."

God Nancy loved that girl.

Nancy stood and they started back down the path together. "Well, I think the first thing we need to do is talk to Beth. See if it's something she would even want."

Thomas nodded. "I think it should be you who talks to her."

"I'll see her tomorrow. I can talk to her about it then. I don't think she has too many options. She can't move back home unless she finds a decent teaching job and last time she checked, it wasn't looking good." Nancy couldn't imagine if she had been far from home when Sam died. If she hadn't been able to move in with her dad, she would have been screwed. "We just need to help her."

Thomas patted her shoulder as the woods closed back in around them. "We will. She'll be okay. She's a strong girl."

Nancy didn't want Beth to be okay. She was okay and it sucked.

She wanted Beth to be happy. Like Mina.

"I hope so."

They stayed quiet as they made their way back down the trail. His downhill steps were clearly easier. It took them half the time to get back down that it did to get up. "You're looking pretty good there."

Thomas shrugged. "It's hard to tell anymore. I just keep trying." He pulled out his phone and checked the time. "I gotta go. I told Mina I'd come help her with a few things at the house and then we could go to lunch."

"At least somebody gets to go to lunch with her." With Mina working on a tight schedule there was much less time for their lunch dates.

Thomas grinned. "It's nice to know I pull at least a little weight."

He wrapped Nancy in a hug. "I'll call ya later."

"Okay honey." She got in her car and started the engine, knowing he wouldn't leave until she did.

Nancy flipped on the radio as she drove home. Every breath she took felt deeper than the last. She looked at her reflection in the mirror. The smile on her face surprised her.

After the difficult conversations she'd just had with Thomas she would expect to feel sad, depressed, even angry. She didn't.

She felt... light.

Maybe even a little relaxed. It could be the relief of finally confessing a few of the mistakes she'd made in her life or it could be the exercise and fresh air. Either way, she felt good.

Really good.

Maybe Thomas was right. Maybe Beth would come out of all of this and be better than fine.

Maybe she would too. Hell if she wasn't going to try.

By the time she got home, Nancy was mentally planning another girl's night. And another trip to the park. If she was going to fix this mess she'd made of her life, that place might have the perfect combination of physical activity and calm quiet for her to figure out how.

She pulled into her driveway and immediately hit the brakes, the positivity and excitement she'd gained evaporating instantly, like drops of water in a hot skillet.

There was a car in her driveway. A car she knew well. Along with the man who'd owned it for over thirty years.

Standing in her driveway, beside a bright orange GTO, was Paul.

SEVEN

PAUL STOOD IN Nancy's house for the first time in well over thirty years. The place was dramatically different than the farmhouse he remembered. Much more... feminine.

"Um." Nancy looked at him then quickly looked away to hang her jacket on a hook by the front door and slip her shoes off onto the matt directly under it. "Do you want coffee?"

"If you have it made." Paul stood at the front door, his work boots fused to the throw rug protecting the lightly colored hardwood floors. Those, he remembered staring down at while Nancy's dad eyed him from his easy chair in the corner. They looked exactly the same as they did when he was a seventeen-year-old kid ready to shit his pants in fear.

Everything else though...

Everything else was completely different. The worn, simple furniture was gone. In its place were a number of large couches and chairs that filled the large space perfectly. The six-foot console cabinet that held a record player and television when John was alive was replaced by a sturdy antique chest with drawers and topped with a flat-screen. In place of the braided rugs, faded with age and abuse from dusty boots, were shaggy, oatmeal colored carpets, one under the couches and one on the other side of the room in front of a large cabinet beneath two extra-wide armchairs.

In spite of all the differences, the place looked exactly as he imagined it would. From the lace curtains to the dirty work boots by the door, the house was a perfect reflection of its owner. Soft and tough at the same time.

Only he was beginning to wonder if maybe the owner wasn't as tough as he'd always thought. It was that newly planted suspicion that kept him up all night then dragged him here today.

"It's not, but I could use some too." Nancy turned and went to the kitchen, her socked feet barely whispering across the floor as she went.

The floors were spotless, hell the whole damn house was immaculate. Perfectly clean, perfectly organized, thus leaving him unsure about his boots. Looking down at them again he tipped the soles to the ceiling to see what sort of random construction crap might be jammed in between the treads.

"It's okay."

He looked up to find her propped in the kitchen doorway, watching him, the sound of steadily dripping liquid reaching him mere seconds before the scent of freshly brewing beans joined the soft vanilla hanging in the air.

That was what he always expected Nancy to smell like. Sweet like vanilla, rich like coffee, and familiar.

Like home.

"You can leave them on." She smiled slightly.

"Okay." Paul stayed put anyway and tried to work through the things he wanted to say. The reasons he came here were quickly moving to the back of his mind behind lace curtains and perfect scents and...

Her.

But it had to stop. He had to stop. He was here for her. To release her from whatever guilt she carried about him and what happened. Then, most importantly, he had to set boundaries.

And that was what he was going to do. For her. For Mina.

And selfishly, for him.

REGRET

Nancy watched him intently for a second before slowly turning back into the kitchen. He heard gentle clinking and a few seconds later she emerged with two cups. Wisps of steam curled up from the freshly brewed coffee as she carefully walked toward him.

"Do you want to sit down?" She tipped her head to the center of the room where two deep rose sofas and coordinating floral print chairs were situated in a little cluster facing the general direction of the television where it backed up against the same wall that opened into the kitchen.

"Sure." Paul waited for her to select a seat in one of the chairs before sitting across from her in the middle of one of the couches. It was softer than it looked and the weight of his six four frame sank low into the plush upholstery.

Nancy looked down. "Oh, sorry." She leaned deeply across the low rectangular table he'd strategically placed between them, holding out one cup of coffee. "This is yours."

His eyes dragged down the length of her neck, hanging on the drape of her sweater as it gaped away from her body giving him a glimpse of pale blue lace running along the swell of her breast. The same breast burned into his memory as if he'd touched it a million times.

He took the cup from her and swallowed a scalding hot mouthful trying desperately to refocus his thoughts. Now was not the time to get distracted by his nonsensical feelings, especially ones like that. He was here for one reason and that was Nancy.

"Are you feeling okay?" Nancy's voice was soft, hesitant.

Paul rubbed one hand across his mouth and jaw line, regretting not taking a minute to look in the mirror before leaving his house. He must look like shit. Considering he hadn't slept last night, the look of regret and pain etched in Nancy's face haunting him every time he closed his eyes, it would make sense.

He always believed when Nancy walked away from him she'd never looked back. It was an easy assumption. Every woman since her had done it. Easily.

Oh sure, he'd imagined differently. Sometimes he even let himself believe her smiles and waves when they passed in town were more than simply her kind nature. But the truth was always there to quickly bring him back to his senses.

But last night.

Last night was threatening his hold on the truth and he was here to get his grip back. This time it might have to be a stranglehold.

"Nan, I'm sorry about last night."

She laughed out loud.

That wasn't the reaction he'd been expecting, but it should have been.

He was an idiot. Once again, reading more into her actions than was actually there. Stupid. He was so stupid. Even after all this time he still didn't want to believe the truth even as it slapped him in the face.

"What in the world do you think you have to be sorry for?" She looked shocked, which shocked him in return, making him doubt his doubts and sending his head spinning.

"You were upset and I..." He raked his hands through his hair as he struggled to keep up with what was actually going on between them right now. "I should have been nicer."

Nancy leaned back on the couch and studied him. Her eyes moved across his face with an intensity that made him want to squirm.

"I can't imagine why you would want to be nice to me at all." Her voice caught at the end of her statement. Just barely, but it echoed through him filling his body with certainty.

And dread.

He was right the first time. She was upset. What happened between them did matter to her.

For the first time it dawned on him this new reality might be more difficult to handle than the truth he'd been living with for thirty years. All this time he'd known Nancy didn't want him. If that wasn't really the case...

Paul swallowed hard and focused on suffocating the part of him that sprang to life at the possibility. He needed to keep it together right now. This didn't change anything. "What happened between us was a very long time ago. We were kids. Kids make mistakes."

Nancy raised an eyebrow at him. "Do you think us not ending up together was a mistake?"

Paul froze as he realized what he'd said, his bottom lip pressed against his coffee cup. Her eyes were locked on him as she waited for his answer. He set the cup down and rubbed his hands over his face. Shit.

"Please. Tell me. I need to know." She reached across the table and gently touched his arm. "Please."

His attention narrowed to where her hand rested against his body. The heat from her palm seeped through his flannel shirt. What in the hell was it about this woman? Just the feel of her hand on his arm could completely scramble his thoughts and steal all coherence from his mind.

"I just meant kids do stupid things and don't really think of how it affects other people. All kids do it."

He thought of the women he'd known since her. "Hell, some adults still do it."

"Do you hate me?"

His head snapped up to look at her. "No. How could I hate you?" Words fell from his mouth before he could filter them. "I would never hate you."

"Then why--" She closed her eyes and took a deep breath. He could see her throat move as she swallowed. She took one quick breath before opening her eyes. "Then why do you act the way you do around me?"

He straightened as much as he could on the overstuffed couch. "What do you mean?"

Sure he'd been brisk with her. He had to be. But he never thought it was more than that, certainly not enough to make her think he could hate her.

"Like you can't wait to get away from me." She clamped her mouth tightly shut as soon as the statement cleared her lips.

Damn.

It was because he *couldn't* wait to get away from her. Being close to her was the worst form of torture he could think of. Hell, it had taken him hours to work up the courage to come here today, knowing he would be alone with her and, lucky him, it was turning out to be as agonizing as he expected.

Just being in the same room as her was awful but this was worse. She was so close. So beautiful. So perfect. He could smell her perfume, her shampoo, even the lotion on her hands. He wanted to bury his face in her neck, breathe it all in so he would never forget it. Hold her in his arms just once so he would at least know how it felt.

But there were a million reasons he couldn't do that, even now that she might want him to, and he decided to focus on one of the less embarrassing ones.

Nancy had been through a lot in the past few months. Horrible, awful things had happened and it would be wrong of him to capitalize on her fragile state. A good man didn't take advantage of a woman who was hurting. A woman in pain. And he was going to be a good man to her. She deserved that.

"I…" He made the mistake of looking up. Nancy's eyes were shimmering and pink at the edges, breaking his heart and blurring his judgment. "I don't trust myself around you."

Those were not the words he intended to say and he regretted them immediately.

She blinked a few times. "I don't understand."

He should never have come here. He was only making things worse. This was a perfect example of why he tried to stay away from her. He couldn't lie to her and he didn't want to tell the truth, but he was running out of options. Quickly.

They loved the same people and wanted them in their lives. That meant he had to come up with a solution that would preserve his sanity. No matter what she said or what he hoped she was thinking, he had to do what was best. For them both.

"Nan, it is what it is." He had to reach deep for the next words, knowing they would be sealing his fate. "Maybe we can find a way to at least be friends.

He stood up. It was done and it was time to leave. Quickly, before his mouth kept running.

Unfortunately, Nancy was not as done with their conversation as he was. She immediately stepped into his path, blocking him and resting her hand in the middle of his chest.

He sucked in his breath and looked up at the ceiling, trying to focus on anything but her nearness.

"Paul."

He held his breath as he worked up the gumption to step away from her touch. He knew he had to move but it felt impossible, as if there was a magnetic pull with the strength of an ox emitting from her palm.

He sucked in a breath and lowered his gaze to find her smiling up at him.

"I would love to be friends with someone like you." She stepped forward and before he had a chance to realize what was happening, wrapped her arms around him and pressed her body tightly against his in a hug.

But not a friendly hug.

Friendly hugs were ass out, faces turned away with back patting. This was about as far from that as you could get.

He could feel every inch of her against him. Arms, chest, belly, legs. All of it. Then she pulled closer and demolished any remaining willpower he had. His arms went around her waist, his palms flattened on her back

He tucked his head closer to hers, feeling the strands of her hair snag in his beard. She fit against him perfectly. He felt like a giant around most women, but Nancy was tall. Probably close to five ten which made the top of her head fall just above his chin and let her face tuck perfectly into the crook of his neck.

He could hear the blood in his veins as it picked up speed. The feel of her soft breath against the sensitive skin of his neck made his heart rate spike.

He wanted to hold her like this forever, but he couldn't.

He gently stepped out of her embrace, but only barely, not wanting to give up the closeness just yet.

"I need to go."

Nancy nodded, rubbing her lips together, drawing his attention to her mouth. "You said you don't hate me, but…" She looked up at him, the lips he watched so closely mere inches away from his. "Do you think you will ever be able to forgive me?"

"I forgave you a long time ago."

After the sting of her rejection wore off, he realized he couldn't blame her. Sam was the guy every girl wanted. He was the good looking captain of the football team, his folks were well off and he was one hell of a charmer. Not many women turned him down, even after he was married.

She chewed her lip.

How long had it been since she'd been kissed? How long had it been since-

He grabbed the door handle behind his back and yanked it open to escape onto the porch. As he backed toward the steps, Nancy appeared in the doorway.

"Maybe I'll see you soon?"

Oh God he hoped not.

EIGHT

"NANA! I POOPED."

Liza had been in the bathroom for ten minutes while she was trying to turn over the laundry. If the three-year-old wasn't spending the time pooping there would have been a problem. A watery, soapy, messy problem.

Like last week. If there was one requirement for watching Beth's youngest, it was surveillance. Lots of it.

"I'm coming honey." Nancy set the cycle on the washer and pushed start before grabbing the basket of clean clothes she'd just tumbled out of the dryer to head through the kitchen and across the front of the house to the half-bath where Liza was sitting on the pot, her little legs dangling, reading the Farmer's Almanac she found on the sink.

Nancy laughed as she set the basket beside the door and folded a few squares of toilet paper. "You feel better?"

"Oh yes. Now I have room for lunch." The little girl jumped off the toilet and climbed onto the stool at the sink. "I didn't touch my butt, but I'll wash my hands anyways."

Nancy pumped lavender scented soap onto their hands and scrubbed them together, rubbing each little fingertip then rinsing them off. She grabbed the hand towel off the hook and struggled to dry Liza's hands as she took off into the living room, launching herself onto the couch to finish watching the cartoon flashing across the screen.

If there was one good thing to come of the past few months of sadness, it was finally being a part of Liza and Kate's lives. Nancy always assumed Beth simply preferred to be with her parents. It hurt a little, but she could understand Beth not really considering her the girls' grandmother. Technically, she was their aunt. Great aunt at that.

It was only after Rich died that Nancy found out the real reason Beth avoided her and it broke her heart.

Maybe if she'd known their marriage was troubled from the beginning she could have helped. All those years Beth needed someone and was too worried about Nancy taking Rich's side to ask.

But now Nancy had the chance to be there for her. Beth needed her now more than ever and to be honest, Nancy needed her too. She'd lost Rich in more ways than one. Getting to spend time with his girls helped her remember the good in him, reassured her it really was there at some point.

She picked up the basket and headed upstairs. "Nana will be right back and then it will be time to go get your sister."

"I can stay here and watch this."

Nancy sighed and bent down to peek through the top rail. "We can pause your show and you can watch it later."

Liza's eyes were glued to the television and she was fully engrossed in whatever princess was prancing around the screen. Nancy sighed and headed the rest of the way up the stairs.

She was keeping the girls three days a week and quickly discovering while girls were a bit different, kids were mostly all the same. They all touched their butts and lied about it then ignored you when the TV was on.

Occasionally though, they surprised you. Like the day Liza figured out how to open the gun cabinet.

Nancy quickly put away the clothes and stacked the basket with the others she kept in the spare bedroom. Her laundry had doubled since she'd been babysitting. Mostly towels and shirts. It never failed. If there was anything on either of the little mess makers, inevitably, it ended up on her.

It was wonderful.

She checked her watch as she headed back down the stairs. They had ten minutes to get on the road. Kate was in morning kindergarten which meant she and Beth could go in together in the morning and Nancy just had to pick her up right before lunch. Then they got to spend a few hours together before Beth was finished with her third grade class and came to get the girls.

Many nights she even stayed for dinner.

"Come on Li. We need to get your shoes on." She grabbed the white Mary Jane's off the end table.

"I don't wanna go. I'm big now. I can stay here while you go." She tucked her feet under her butt. "Daddy let me and Kate stay home when he went to the store cause he was thirsty."

Nancy's stomach dropped. She took a deep breath and tried to push the statement to the back of her mind. She could be upset about it later.

It didn't matter anymore anyway.

"Well, I would be lonely without you." She gave Liza a sad look. It wasn't too hard to do, considering.

The little girl sighed dramatically and stretched her legs out so Nancy could slip on her shoes.

Liza sang loudly in the backseat as they drove into town toward the elementary school. These three days a week were turning out to be some of her favorite times, ever.

Looking back, she'd never been able to enjoy Thomas and Rich like this. There was so much else going on around them making life difficult and frustrating and sad. Very, very sad.

Some of it she wouldn't change, even if she could. Other things, like Rich's mom taking off, were a different story. Maybe if Carol stayed, Rich would have been different. Maybe he would still be here and be happy and healthy.

Nancy blinked hard as she pulled into the school pick-up line. She tried her best to only be happy around the girls. They didn't need any more sadness in their life.

By the time she was at the front of the line, the lump in her throat was almost gone. Seeing Kate's face light up when she saw her, made it disappear completely.

The little girl yanked the door open and climbed into her booster seat beside her sister. "Nana I am so hungry." She clicked her belt into place. "Do we have to drive all the way back to your house for lunch?"

"Hmmmm." Nancy pulled away from the curb, looking carefully for any rogue kindergarteners straying from the sidewalk. "What are you thinking?"

"I would really like a hamburger." Kate swiped at her forehead, trying to push a few loose hairs clinging to her skin. Her cheeks were flushed from running around during recess and bouncing in line for pick-up.

"I want French fries." Liza flapped her feet up and down in her car seat. "I'm so hungry too."

French fries did sound pretty good. Mina was pretty close to town and the diner was her favorite...

Nancy grabbed her phone while they were stopped at the light waiting to pull out of the school lot. Mina picked up on the first ring.

"Hey. How's it going?"

"Good. Want to grab lunch at the diner?" Nancy glanced in the mirror at the girls who were poking each other and giggling.

"Yes. Yes I do. I'll be there in five minutes."

Nancy was already parking when they hung up. She looked in the rearview mirror. "You ladies hungry?"

"Yes!"

Kate had her belt off and was trying to help Liza with hers by the time Nancy was out of the car and opening the back door. She undid the car seat harness and hoisted Liza out before grabbing Kate's hand. She used her hip to close the door and they crossed the lot to the diner.

They were just barely situated in the booth when Mina slid in beside Kate. The little girl grinned at her. "I wanted to sit by you."

Mina dropped her purse on the seat beside her. "Thank goodness, because I wanted to sit by you too." She wrapped her arm around Kate's shoulders and leaned into a hug. Kate scrunched up her nose and wriggled away.

"You're cold."

Mina groaned. "That house is going to make me crazy." She looked pointedly at Nancy. "Unless Paul manages it first."

Nancy couldn't help herself. "He does have a way of doing that doesn't he?"

Mina pursed her lips but not before Nancy saw her mouth start to tug into a smile. The younger woman picked up a menu and held it up, blocking Nancy's view of her face. "Are we ever gonna talk about that?"

Now it was Nancy's turn to groan. "Maybe. But not today. You could say I'm feeling the same as you."

Mina dropped her menu, her facial expressions obviously back in check. "Fair enough. Let's eat French fries then. That fixes everything."

Liza bounced in the seat beside Nancy. "Milkshakes too."

By the time they finished lunch and Mina was on her way back to the house to work, the afternoon was well underway. It didn't make sense to drive back out to Nancy's house so she and the girls headed to the library where they got Kate signed up for her own library card. The girls ran up and down the aisles collecting books until they each had a stack to borrow.

Nancy texted Beth before they left, letting her know she would drop the girls off to her at the school since they were already in town.

"Where are we going now?" Kate was craning her neck to look out the window.

"I was thinking of picking up a special treat for you and your mommy to have after dinner tonight. Does that sound good?" Nancy turned into the bakery. Maybe a cupcake would tempt Beth. She'd lost so much weight. She'd had a little cushion to spare, but it was more than gone now.

Kate sat quietly in the back seat. Not the reaction she was expecting to get when cake was involved.

"What's wrong sweetheart? Are you tired?" Nothing like a full belly and a fun day to poop a kid out.

"My mommy's sad a lot."

Nancy swallowed hard and took a long slow breath before she was ready to face the girls in the back seat. She turned in her seat. Four big eyes were glued to her face, waiting.

"Do you get sad sometimes?"

Both girls nodded.

"Mommies get sad too." She waited, giving them time to process. This was difficult to understand, even for some adults.

"Can we make her be happy again?" Kate's chin had the smallest quiver as she spoke.

"She will be happy again. I promise. But it's not your job to make your mommy happy." She reached back to squeeze Kate's leg. "Just getting to be your mommy makes her happy."

Kate's mouth twisted into a smile. "That's what she says."

"Because it's the truth." Nancy took a deep breath trying to keep the emotion out of her voice. "Now, let's go get some cupcakes."

"I want cupcakes! They make me happy." Liza clapped as Nancy wrestled her wiggling body out of her car seat.

Hopefully cupcakes could make them all feel a little happier.

****

Paul skimmed his scraper down the drywall doing his best not to let his mind wander, keeping it safely busy working out the schedule he would have to stick to in order to finish this house on time. Unfortunately they might hit a roadblock if he couldn't figure out what in the hell was going on with the furnace.

He was so forcefully engrossed in his planning that the opening of the front door startled him, making him jump and resulting in a divot in the smooth line of mud he was scraping down the drywall seam.

Blowing out a frustrated breath he straightened, moving his neck from side to side, as he walked to the corner of the bedroom. He wasn't a twenty-year-old kid anymore and his body was showing it. In more ways than one.

He raked the dusty chunks stuck to the corner of his trowel into the trash bucket then loaded a fresh dose of the pasty compound and started from the top again. He was halfway down the seam before Mina wandered into the room.

"How was your lunch?"

Mina stepped into his line of vision, her arms crossed and an eyebrow raised. "Decent. Yours?"

He finished the line and moved to the next. "Didn't take one. I want to get this room mudded before the furnace decides to completely quit."

"Do you want me to start mudding the other bedroom?"

Paul stepped back and surveyed the room. "I don't think it's worth the risk. I only have a little left to do here." He scraped his mud into a pile on the tray. "If I'd known the furnace was going to give us fits, I would have held off on this room too."

At this point the best he could do was hope he could keep it warm enough to keep the compound from cracking until the new unit they ordered came in.

Mina stood in the corner watching him quietly. She had something on her mind and it wasn't hard to guess what it was. He kept working, pretending not to notice. Hopefully she would decide it wasn't any of her business and go enjoy the rest of her day.

"I had lunch with Nancy today." She wandered across the room to grab the broom sitting in the corner. A pointless move considering all the drywall dust that would be covering the house in a couple days.

"That's what I figured." He kept moving. The faster he finished, the sooner he would be away from the second woman causing him grief.

Mina blew out a sigh. "I don't understand."

"Nothing to understand." He started the last seam. The end was in sight, but he got impatient and heavy-handed. He scraped the excess off his scraper and smoothed down the line again.

Mina stood right beside him, the broom still in her hand even though she hadn't touched it to the floor since she grabbed it. "You act like you don't give a shit when I know that's not true."

Paul tipped his head back to look at the ceiling. When he found out Mina and Nancy were friends he worried it would be like a carrot on a stick tempting him every day, but always out of his reach.

He could only be so lucky.

He set his tools down on the lid of an unopened five gallon bucket and made sure the lid of the bucket he was using was in place before using his boot to stomp it closed. "It doesn't matter how I feel."

Mina rolled her eyes. "Of course it does."

Paul grabbed his tools and stepped around her. "I don't want to have this conversation with you."

Mina followed behind him as he stalked down the hall toward the kitchen and the only working sink in the house. "Then have it with her."

Paul shook his head as he twisted on the hot water and rinsed off the drywall compound clinging to the blades of his tools. Talking to Nancy yesterday only made things worse. "You don't understand."

"I think you're wrong."

He set the scrapers into the dish rack on the counter beside the sink and turned to her. "I don't care what you think." Grabbing his keys off the counter, he headed to the front door. "I'll come deal with the furnace later."

There was nothing that could keep him in that house another second. Right now he didn't care if the whole damn thing froze and he had to dig out every speck of compound and do it again. It would be better than having to explain himself to someone who couldn't understand even if she tried.

He backed down the driveway and took off not really sure where he was headed. A beer sounded really good right now. Hell, sitting in the bar chatting with the daytime cronies sounded good. Anything besides sitting around thinking of the look on Nancy's face yesterday.

He'd almost kissed her.

When he realized what he was about to do, he took off like a bat out of hell. Unfortunately he wasn't fast enough to miss the way she looked at him.

She didn't seem to realize it was for her own good.

As he drove through town, the heat of the sun warmed the interior of his truck pushing the temperature past a comfortable point. He cracked the window, letting the brisk air blow through the cab.

He felt like he was being shoved between a rock and a hard place. He really didn't want to talk to Mina any more about Nancy. She had the best intentions, but it really wasn't any of her business. Which led him to the hard place. He didn't want to talk to Nancy either.

What he really wanted was for everything to go back the way it was. Unfortunately with Mina involved that probably wasn't going to be an option. She wasn't one to sit back and let things go. She ran head first into whatever problem she had and wrangled it into submission.

And she wasn't his only problem. Nancy didn't seem to be any more willing to let things go.

Paul looked in his rear view mirror and cut the wheel, spinning his truck in a u-turn.

In less than five minutes, his ass was parked on the barstool he'd occupied countless hours over the last thirty-some-odd years. It was like old times, sitting in the dim lighting, leaned against the wood top of the bar, squinting at the ancient box TV shoved into an alcove high on the wall.

"Hey buddy." Ron the daytime bartender ambled his way. "Long time no see. Thirsty?"

Paul nodded.

A few seconds later, Ron set a tall glass of the usual on the bar in front of him. "You been all right man? You look like you lost some weight."

"Just busy." He wrapped his hand around the glass letting the coolness of the amber ale sink into his palm.

Ron nodded back. "Glad to see ya." He slid down the bar to replace another regular's empty bottle.

Paul stared at his beer. It had been months since he'd had a drop of anything other than water and the occasional cola.

For years, this is where he spent most of his Friday and Saturday nights but the visits got a little more frequent after he started working with Mina.

He knew she and Nancy were friends when he took the job, he just never expected Mina would become any more than a temporary employer for him. He also didn't realize exactly how much that girl could talk. Specifically how much she would talk about Nancy.

Now he was stuck dealing with the two women he loved, and they were ganging up on him. Pushing him to talk about things that are better left alone.

"Hey Paulie." One of his favorite bar flies wandered over and sat on the stool beside him, propping his cane against his leg after he was settled. "Where ya been?"

"Just workin'."

"Oh." Old Saul nodded his head slowly before giving him a crinkly eyed wink. "Thought maybe you and Nancy finally figured it out."

Son of a bitch. There was no escaping this shit.

"Nothing to figure out." Paul held his glass up, staring though to the gold tinted scene behind it. He tipped it to his lips, taking a deep breath, pulling the hoppy smell deep into his lungs before taking a sip.

It wasn't as good as he remembered.

The old man laughed beside him. "You're still as big of a dumbass as you were in high school. Letting some pecker take your girl without a fight."

Paul slammed the beer down, foam sloshing over the edge and running down to his hand where it clenched the glass.

"She wasn't mine to take."

"And whose fault is that?"

All the anger and rage came back like it was yesterday. Like he was that seventeen-year-old kid betrayed by his best friend all over again.

Paul wiped his wet hand down the leg of his jeans. It was fucking Sam's fault. All of this was Sam's fault. He was a shitty friend and an even shittier husband. He only asked Nancy out in the first place because he couldn't stand for a woman to want Paul instead of him.

Now it was too late. The best chance Paul had with her was then, when he was young and strong and capable.

And Sam stole it. Made him her second best option, just for spite.

It was time to go.

Paul stood up and gave Saul a pat on the back. "Gotta head out. Good to see you."

He'd only been in the bar a few minutes, but the bright light of the day stung his eyes and made his head hurt. He swiped at his eyes with the sleeve of his lined work shirt, the sour smell of spilled beer still lingering on his hand.

Kicking at the gravel lining the parking lot, his boot sent tiny rocks and dust scattering. He just wanted to be left the fuck alone. Why was it so hard for everyone to mind their own fucking business?

Paul got in his truck, slamming the door. He leaned his head back against the headrest and stared at the ceiling trying to swallow down years of frustration and anger.

REGRET

He started the truck and pulled out of the lot, headed to the only place no one would give him shit. It looked like his world was about to get a whole lot smaller until this all died down.

NINE

NANCY WALKED INTO the dark house.

The dark and cold house.

"Shit." She fished her cell out of the pocket of her sweater and used the flashlight on it to find the light switch just inside the door. Flipping it on, she went in search of the thermostat.

Forty-five degrees.

That was bad news. She turned off the beam of light emitting from her cell, then dialed Thomas' number.

"Hello?" He practically yelled into the phone and even then the shouts of the crowd around him threatened to drown him out.

"I think it's totally out." Nancy squinted at the dial to make sure it was set properly. For some stupid reason she tapped on the face of the temperature gauge. Like that was going to do anything. It didn't take a rocket scientist to tell it was freaking cold in here.

Yesterday it seemed like the warm weather was finally coming, but once again Mother Nature proved herself to be a tease and her ill temperament was about to make a big mess for Mina.

And Paul.

"I was afraid of that." She heard the rumble of Thomas' voice as he spoke away from the phone speaker. He, Mina and Charlie were watching Maddie finish out the club volleyball season. Nancy was too, until Mina told her they were having problems with the furnace and would have to go past the house after the game to make sure it was warm enough to dry the mud on the walls.

"Thanks for checking. I guess we'll head over there and set up space heaters after we're done here."

"Why can't I just do that now? I'm already here." That was the whole reason she left Maddie's game, so they didn't have to drag around two tired, hungry kids at nine o'clock on a school night.

"The heaters aren't there."

Nancy was fishing her keys out of her pocket and walking back out the front door. "Where are they? I'll just go get them."

"You don't have to do that."

"I'm already in the car, are they in the garage?" She backed down the driveway, intent on heading to Mina's house.

"They're at Paul's."

****

The doorbell rang, interrupting the fly fishing show he'd switched on before whipping up his gourmet dinner. Less than two minutes ago he'd parked his ass on the leather reclining couch, a plate full of bologna sandwich and Cheetos perched on his lap. After a morning of fighting the furnace into submission and an afternoon of mudding, he was ready to relax.

And now someone was at his door and they were ringing the bell. Again.

Dropping the paper plate on the dark cherry end table at his elbow, he wrestled the footrest down and heaved himself up. Unless it was a uniformed little girl offering cookies, whoever was on the other side of that door was about to be real sorry they were screwing with his night.

He yanked open the door, not even taking the time to peek and see who it was. Hopefully he'd scare the shit out of him and they'd take off running before his show was back from the commercial break.

He glared through the open door for half a second before realization set in, dragging a healthy dose of shock along with it.

Unfortunately, his late night visitor didn't look the least bit scared of him.

Nancy raised an eyebrow. "Is this how you greet all your guests?" A smile quirked the edge of her lips. "Or just your friends?"

He swallowed and tried to find words to say. Never in a million years would he have expected this. Her, showing up unannounced, a smile on her face, as if she knew what she was doing to him.

And liked it.

The fear that accompanied that possibility left him in an embarrassing state. One in which he simply stood in his sock feet, mouth agape, staring at the woman interrupting his fishing show.

Hell, she was interrupting his whole damn life.

And damned if she didn't look good while she did it. She wore jeans that clung to every curve of her body and a white low-cut shirt tucked into the waistband. All that protected her from the chill of the night was a long, loose black and white sweater.

He blinked trying to break the spell she had on him. Finally he found his voice. "What are you doing here?"

Her eyebrows drew together. "Mina said she texted you."

He had no idea where his phone was. It wasn't unusual. He never knew where he left the damn thing once he got home and took off the clip that held it to his waistband while he worked. Drop one in a bucket of cement once and you figure out a way to avoid doing it again.

"The furnace is out at the house. They're at Maddie's game so I told them I would take the heaters over and set them up." Nancy's eyes wandered around the gap between his body and the doorframe, looking into the house behind him. "Can I come in? It's really cold."

He needed to be slapped. He was an ass. What in the hell was wrong with him?

"Yeah." He stepped to one side. "Come in. I'm sorry. I was just a little surprised."

Her hands rubbed up and down her arms as she stepped past him into the foyer. "I'm sorry. I thought you would be expecting me." Only a couple steps in, she stopped and stood silently as her eyes roamed what she could see of the house.

"It's beautiful Paul." She gently touched the woodwork framing the doorway into the vaulted great room. "How long have you lived here?"

He rubbed one hand across the back of his neck, a little uncomfortable with her praise of his house and a lot uncomfortable with her being in it. "Almost two years now."

She stepped further into his home, her head tipping back to take in the beams of the soaring ceiling. "What did it look like when you bought it?"

"It was pretty bad, but…"

Nancy looked back at him from where she stopped to study a watercolor painting hanging on the wall, her fingers gently tracing the heavy wood frame. "But what?"

Paul swallowed. This was much harder than he expected it to be. He loved talking about his house, the way he fixed it up, but it was a struggle to make words come out. The sight of her, in his house. In his life.

It was what he'd wanted, what he'd dreamed of for years and now that it was happening, he wanted it to stop.

It was too good. Too perfect. Too easy. Being with her in the quiet of his house instead of sitting alone pretending to watch television. It felt real.

He started to sweat.

"Paul? Are you okay?" Her brows came together as she watched him closely. "You got really pale."

He shook his head. "I'm fine." It was time to take back his night. Maybe it would be the first step to regaining his life. "You go home. I'll handle the heaters."

Nancy didn't seem to hear him. She was moving through his house, touching the walls, the furniture. Even the countertops in his kitchen. "I can't believe how gorgeous this place is." Her voice was filled with awe and a touch of shock which hurt what little ego he had left. If he was good at anything it was fixing houses.

"You imagined me living like a desolate bachelor?" He padded through the great room and to the dining area where he grabbed his coat off the back of a chair.

Nancy nodded to his forgotten supper. "You eat like one."

He looked at the pale white bread and neon colored curls beside it. "Fair enough." He nodded to the door. "I mean it. You go home. No reason for you to be freezing." He glanced back at her extremely complimentary but also ill-considered outfit. "Why are you even out in this weather without a coat?"

Nancy looked down and wrapped her sweater across her front like it would make it look warmer. "I didn't realize what all the evening would entail."

"All the more reason for you to go home." He stepped toward her, hoping it would push her closer to the front of the house and closer to the door.

Much to his dismay, she held firm, crossing her arms and shaking her head. "No. I'm going with you."

Holy hell this woman was stubborn. "You'll freeze."

She gave him a sly smile. "Not if you give me a coat to wear."

They stared at each other, Nancy still smiling, him trying to at least feel like he put up some sort of fight even though he knew what was going to happen. He was going to give her what she wanted. Mostly because that's all he'd ever wanted to do.

Give the woman everything she wanted and everything she deserved. At one point in his life maybe he could have. Not now.

But that didn't stop him from wanting.

He held the coat in his hand out to her. "Come on."

The space heaters were in the garage. He grabbed another coat from the closet, sliding it on as he opened the door into the heated space where he kept his baby.

"Holy cow." Nancy stepped in behind him, zipping his Carhart up to her chin.

He tried not to notice the feeling of possession chewing on his brain at the sight of her in his coat. He also chose to ignore the satisfaction he felt deep inside knowing that he was the one to take care of her tonight.

"This is as nice as the house." She pointed to a small room framed into one corner. "Is that a bathroom?" She laughed. The sound bounced off the walls around him, making him smother a smile. "This place is fantastic."

Opening a set of bi-fold doors, he started lining up heaters. There was no time to waste. Nancy needed to go home so he could try to find his way back to reality. The one where she isn't standing in his house, wrapped in his coat, praising the skills he's most proud of, making him think impossible thoughts.

The worst part was they didn't seem so impossible right now. And that was why he needed to hurry this up. Before he completely lost his mind and started thinking he could have her. That he could make her completely happy in spite of—

The sound of the garage door opening startled him. His head flipped around to find Nancy walking away from the button and grabbing a heater. She straightened and walked past him to the now open door.

"We're putting these in your truck right?"

He grabbed two and followed behind her. "Yeah."

He dropped his into the bed of the truck and opened the driver's door to start the engine and crank up the heat. "Get in. I'll load the rest."

She was already on her way back to the garage, but paused. "Okay." She walked to the passenger side and opened the door, chewing her lip as she went then slowly turned and looked right at him, her eyes soft. "Thank you."

Ten minutes later they were pulling up in front of the other house. It was a short ride, but long enough to have his nerves frayed. The blower of the heater rolled the sweet smell of her through the cab of his truck, making her presence hard to ignore no matter how hard he tried.

Stepping into the cold night was a welcome relief. A deep, cleansing, breath of frigid air that smelled of dead leaves and freezing dew, and he was ready to tackle the rest of this whole...

He didn't even know what the hell to call this night.

Nancy swept past him, her keys out and jingling in her hand. "I'll open the house up and get the lights on." She didn't wait for an answer, not that he was planning on giving one.

He grabbed two of the six heaters and went inside. She was right. The furnace was out and the high efficiency unit he special ordered wasn't set to come in for a few more days.

"If this doesn't work what will happen?" Nancy flipped on the hall light and continued toward the bedrooms.

He followed behind her. The bedrooms needed the heat most. If they didn't warm up, the mud could crack, setting them back a week. A week they didn't have. The excavation crew was set to start on Thomas' house in two weeks and he would need every bit of that to be finished here and ready to be on site.

"I'll have a lot of work to do." He set the first two space heaters in the back bedroom and plugged them in on opposite sides before flipping them on to the highest setting. He checked the seams for any signs the cold was already doing damage.

So far so good, but the house was cold and only getting colder. He quickly unloaded the last four heaters and set them up in the rest of the rooms that needed heat most. Before heading out, he turned off the water at the main and opened the faucets. The only thing worse than redoing the mud would be redoing a flooded house.

By the time they pulled back into his driveway, the oddity of having Nancy in his truck was wearing off. He no longer noticed her scent floating around him. Unfortunately, her presence in his life was gaining some normalcy and that could be a very dangerous thing for him.

He jumped out of the truck, needing to put some distance back between them. "Thanks. I'll see you later."

But Paul had no intention of seeing her later, or any time after that. Only a fool would let himself fall into the pit in front of him. Especially one who'd been there before.

"Wait." She ran up behind him, stopping too close. "I need to give you your coat."

He backed up, turning away. "It's still cold. I'll get it later." He didn't pause again until he opened the screen door and shoved his key in the lock. The door opened and he was greeting with the familiar smell of home.

And Nancy's lingering perfume.

"Shit." He threw his keys on the entry table and unzipped his coat. The doorbell rang, the soft chiming echoing through the house.

If her damn car wouldn't start he was going to lose it. He pulled the door open and once again it was Nancy standing on his porch, an apologetic smile on her face. "I left my phone on the counter."

He let her in and shut the door behind her. She went to the kitchen and returned, phone in hand, stopping in the still dark entry less than two feet away. He wanted to back up, but running from this problem wasn't doing him any good so his feet stayed planted, holding their ground.

Nancy took a step forward making him immediately regret his decision to stay put. Before he had the chance to decide whether or not to retreat, Nancy's body was pressed against his, along with her lips. His lungs seized as his brain struggled with the realization of what was happening.

His mind was racing in time with his pulse. Her hands traveled up his chest and her fingers trailed along his neck before forking into his hair.

He knew he should stop her. Send her home where she belonged before he didn't want to give himself that option.

But it was already too late.

Her lips were so soft against his as her breath tickled the hair covering his cheek. She leaned in pulling him closer and making him forget everything that was important.

He wrapped his arms around her back and cradled her head in one hand as he took his first taste of her, sweeping his tongue into her open mouth. She sighed against him and her body seemed to soften, melting against his. He held her tighter as he nipped at the fullness of her lips.

His hands ran through her hair as he covered her mouth with his, taking control of what she'd started. He tried to memorize the feel of her body against his. Her taste. The smoothness of her lips. Kissing Nancy was a moment he'd dreamed of for as long as he could remember and he wanted to burn as much into his memory as he could get. In case it never happened again.

It shouldn't be happening now.

Realization hit him like a punch in the gut. What was he doing?

He dropped his arms and tried to step back. She needed to go home. And he needed a kick in the ass.

Her arms squeezed tighter around his neck and she pulled back to look in his eyes. "No."

"No, what?" He tried to take a step back, move away from her gaze, but she stepped with him keeping her body pressed tightly to his.

She was strong. Stronger than he would have guessed a woman could be before he met Mina and saw firsthand how physically capable she was. Based on the grip she had on him, it looked like Nancy could give Mina a run for her money.

"Kiss me again." She brushed her lips gently across his. "I've waited so long for this. Please."

Her voice was so soft, her breath so sweet against his face. He wrapped her in his arms and did as she asked. He kissed her face, her neck, her lips, her hair. He tasted her soft and silky skin as he ran his lips and his tongue up her neck.

For the first time in months, he felt drunk. His head was swimming as he took full advantage of her request.

She met him, kiss for kiss, clinging to him, holding on for dear life. All his reasons for staying away from her, gone. All he had was here and now with the only woman he'd ever really wanted, pressed against him.

Pulling back, he looked down into the woman holding him like she never wanted to let go.

Her face was flushed, the skin around her mouth red and irritated from the roughness of the whiskers he'd neglected for the past two weeks. Rubbing one hand over his jaw, a pang of guilt nagged at his gut and it was all over. Reality once again crashed in around him and he loosened the grip his other arm had on her.

Nancy had to leave before he did something even more stupid like asking her to stay. That was a can of worms he didn't want to open. Couldn't open even if he wanted to.

"Go home Nan." He opened the door and all but shoved her out.

If she stayed any longer Nancy would surely notice something wasn't doing what it should. It hadn't in a couple years. He'd already lost control of his life and most of his sanity, he at least wanted to keep his pride.

What was left of it.

TEN

NANCY PULLED INTO a shaded spot at the edge of the parking lot. Hopefully if she kept the car out of the sun, the chocolates she picked up for the girls Easter baskets wouldn't melt before she got back.

She stepped out into the warm, breezy day. Finally, a beautiful and reasonably warm day. It was desperately needed.

Closing her eyes, she breathed the spring smell of new green deep into her lungs and tried to relax. Retail therapy with the girls hadn't helped, although it did result in a pretty pair of sandals and the pedicure required to wear them.

That hadn't occurred to her. She bent over and gingerly ran a fingertip across the shiny crimson nail of her big toe. It felt dry so hopefully that meant she wouldn't end up with bits of crusty leaf matter stuck in her polish. Even if she did, it would be worth it. Nothing helped her in the way hiking did.

After coming to this park with Thomas, she couldn't wait to come back. It quickly became her sanctuary. A place to relax and reflect. And boy did she have some reflecting to do, even before she threw herself at Paul.

Zipping her light jacket against the breeze, a smile tugged at her lips at the memory. She probably shouldn't be as proud of it as she was, but...

She couldn't help it.

That was why she was here today. To figure out what in the hell to do next. This wasn't the kind of thing she could discuss with the girls. They wouldn't understand how Paul had to be handled.

She still didn't understand exactly how to handle him. But she was learning.

By the time she was halfway up the heavily inclined trail, Nancy was breathing heavy but so far her pedicure was intact along with her new shoes. The flats weren't necessarily meant to be hiking shoes, but it was just too darn pretty to pass the chance up.

Stepping carefully to avoid any still squishy spots, she picked her way along. So far she'd always stopped at the same field she and Thomas sat in, but today was warm and the sun was so pretty streaming through the still bare tree limbs into the woods, so she decided to keep going.

This part of the trail was steeper, making her trek a little more challenging. Just as she'd decided to turn back, the path leveled out and fed into a clearing that looked out over the rural area below.

Nancy walked to the edge and stood, looking out over what must be miles of farms and forests. She didn't realize just how high the peak here was, it certainly didn't appear this tall when looking at it from below.

With no trees around to block it, the sun shined down, sinking into her back, warming her all the way to the core. The breeze blew gently around her, rustling the last of the fall leaves clinging desperately to the few trees rooted in the sharp edge. For the first time in what felt like forever, Nancy felt like everything would be okay. Like *she* would be okay.

It was a feeling she didn't want to end. A peace deep inside she'd never really known. So she stayed, staring out over the quiet scene below her.

The strangely familiar scene.

Nancy looked closer. The dilapidated white barn at the edge of a vast field of turned dirt. The narrow tree line standing between a livestock pond and the edge of a farmhouse yard. It was pretty as a picture. A picture she'd seen before.

At Paul's house.

It never occurred to her the pictures she found so beautiful would be anything other than standard off-the-rack wall décor. It especially didn't occur to her they could be anything more than a way to fill up wall space.

But now she realized they were much more than that. They were paintings by someone who lived here. Most likely someone Paul knew. Probably knew well.

Suddenly she wasn't so fond of the damn paintings.

She knew Paul dated over the years. Why wouldn't he? He was handsome, hard-working, and kind. But for whatever reason, he'd never gotten married. It made her think maybe none of his relationships were that serious. That important.

But keeping someone's paintings and hanging them in your home where you can look at them every day? That sounded more than serious.

That could be love.

Maybe Paul was acting weird around her because he was actually still in love with someone else.

Nancy turned away from the now ruined scene and stalked back down the hill, jealousy egging her on. Anger that she was jealous pushing her faster. So fast, that she forgot to be careful and stuck the pristine toe of her new sandal under a lifted tree root mostly obscured by dried vegetation.

If only the hill wasn't so steep, she wouldn't have been moving fast enough to propel her forward. If only she hadn't been avoiding the soggy spots, she wouldn't have been so close to the drop off.

But she was. And over she went, tumbling down the semi-wooded hill, Princess Bride style, screaming the whole way. She rolled for what felt like forever, sticks jabbing at her ribs, leaves tangling in her hair, until finally the drop leveled out and she came to a stop, dizzy and disoriented.

With no Wesley to save her.

****

Paul was nearly across the field when a scream pierced the peaceful day he was so looking forward to enjoying. It sounded like it came from the woods not far ahead of where he was. That was the good news. The bad news was the heavy rustling that accompanied it.

Someone fell over the side of the trail.

He took off running, adrenaline keeping his heavy bag from slowing him down. Staying along the edge, he looked down the heavily sloping drop as he went, keeping his eyes out for any indication of where to look.

Halfway up the trail he finally saw a figure sprawled about thirty feet down, partially covered with leaves and spewing explicatives.

"Son-of-a-Goddammed mother—"

"Nan?" He stopped and watched as she groaned and covered her face with her arms.

"No."

Paul was halfway down the hill when she sat up. By the time he got to her, Nancy was picking clumps of damp leaf matter out of her hair and glaring at him. "I said no."

He started laughing. "I heard." At least her sense of humor was intact. That was a good sign. "You okay?" He set his bag and folding stool and easel on the ground before crouching down beside her.

She waved him away. "I'm fine. You go back to—" She looked at his discarded painting supplies. "You've got to be kidding me." She dropped her head into her hands. "You're the painter."

"Did you hit your head?" She wasn't making any sense. Without thinking Paul gently tangled his fingers in her hair and slowly felt around for signs of an injury.

Nancy's eyes slowly closed and she let out a breath. "Maybe. I'm not sure. You should check really well just in case."

She relaxed into his hands as he carefully checked every inch of her skull. It wasn't until he was almost done that he realized she was fine, but if she was going to give him an excuse to touch her, well then.

He might as well take it, just this once. It's not like he wasn't already in way over his head because of this woman. What's a little deeper?

Nancy shifted a little in the pile of debris that rolled down the hill with her. She winced.

He stopped. "Did I hurt you?" Maybe she was injured. Maybe he was taking advantage of an impaired woman. It would figure.

"No, my head's fine." She pulled away from his touch to shift her right foot up and quickly tucked it under her left knee, her face growing white.

"What's wrong?" He looked down where she held her ankle, the rest of her foot hidden under her thigh. "Is your ankle okay?"

She shifted again and made a face. "I think I twisted it."

He held out his hand. "Can I see it?"

Nancy shook her head eyes wide, face pale.

He dropped his head to one side in frustration. "Come here and let me see it."

Her head shook faster. "Oh I'm sure it's fine."

He sat down. "Come here. We need to look at it and make sure it's not broken." He hoped the look on his face made it clear to her he wasn't going to drop this.

She sighed. "It's really not that big of a deal. It's just a toe."

"You said it was your ankle."

Nancy dropped her head back, mumbling under her breath. Finally she shoved her injured foot in his direction. "Fine."

There, pointing off to one side, hanging over the edge of her sandal, was an already purple pinky toe. Paul gently inspected foot, looking carefully as he softly pressed around the base of her obviously broken toe before moving on to her rapidly swelling ankle.

"I think I need to lie down." Nancy's already white face went completely colorless as she flopped back onto the ground, draping one arm across her face.

"I've gotta put it back in place."

She shot up as he gripped her toe between his fingers. Before she could stop him, he pulled hard resetting the toe. Nancy's body made a soft thud as she dropped back into the leaves.

Unconscious.

"Nan." Paul knelt at her side, cupping her clammy face in one hand and laying the other gently on her shoulder. "Nan!"

Her eyes flew open and she tried to sit up but he kept the hand on her shoulder firm.

"You need to lie there for a minute." He smiled. "I kinda expected you to be tougher than this."

She narrowed her eyes at him. "What in the hell Paul? You could have at least warned me."

"I figured you wouldn't let me do it if I gave you the option." He started laughing. "I didn't think you'd pass out on me."

She tried to sit up again, this time making it halfway up before her pinking complexion started to grey again.

"Lie back down before you pass out again." Paul pushed gently on her shoulders.

"I didn't pass out." She poked a finger in his chest as she pushed against his hands, trying to stay upright. "You tried to rip off my toe and the pain made me... made me..."

"Pass out." He pushed harder, managing to get her back down.

She scoffed. "I had to lie down because it hurt."

He laughed. "Okay. Let's say you laid down quickly without realizing it."

"That's right." Her look of satisfaction was short lived. "Wait. No!"

He started laughing harder. She shoved at him hard, tipping him onto the ground beside her. She took the opportunity to get up.

At least she tried to get up.

He caught her just before she hit the ground. "Christ. You are just as stubborn as your daughter-in-law." Having Nancy in his life was turning out to be much more eventful than he ever expected.

"What? What, what?" Her lids fluttered open. She looked from side to side, moving just her eyes. "Shit."

He grinned down at her. "I've gotta set you down while I get situated."

"What do you mean?" She crossed her arms over her chest as he placed her butt on the ground beside the bag he'd dropped earlier.

He slung it over his shoulder then handed her the lightweight folding easel and stool he used outdoors. "You're gonna have to hold these."

She looked at him, her brow furrowed in confusion as she took the items he gave her. "You don't think you're going to--"

She let out a surprised shriek as he lifted her off the ground, bouncing her body slightly to get the proper distribution. If he was going to attempt to be the kind of man who carried an injured woman out of the woods he sure as hell wasn't going to risk dropping her because of a bad grip.

Nancy wrapped her free arm around his neck. "You really don't have to do this."

He raised his eyebrows at her as he picked his way through the flat area that paralleled the path she'd fallen from. "Don't I?"

She shook her head. "No. I'm sure if I wait just a few minutes my ankle will feel better."

Paul glanced down at her rapidly swelling joint. "I disagree."

"Well." Nancy chewed her lip as she looked away from him into the woods. "I feel like an idiot."

He shook his head. "Don't feel like an idiot. That trail is dangerous. I told the city they needed fences on that side years ago."

Nancy licked her lips and took a breath. "It's my fault I fell. I was upset and not paying attention."

"You have a lot to be upset about. You've had some bad things happen to you." He pulled her closer, and slowed his pace. Maybe she needed to talk.

Maybe he could be the one to listen.

"Oh." Her voice was quiet. "Yeah." She took a deep breath. "What about you? What have you been doing for the past thirty years?"

He was disappointed at her change in the conversation and not because he was hoping to be her sounding board, even though he might have been. Mostly, he hated having to admit the less than stellar way he'd spent his life.

"Nothing interesting." He looked straight ahead, hoping she would leave it at that.

"I doubt that." She looked at him, her eyes boring into the side of his face. "I'm sure you went out with plenty of interesting women."

"You would be surprised." Interesting was not the word he would use to describe the woman he'd dated.

"You could have asked me out." The soft breath that was tickling his cheek for the entirety of their walk in the woods stopped abruptly. Nancy Richards was holding her breath, waiting for his answer.

He decided to make her wait, still hoping she would let this be.

It didn't work.

She was unfazed and continued on. "I would have said yes you know." Her hand, initially resting on his shoulder, was now gently stroking his neck.

Finally his truck came into view. He picked up the pace. His arms were wearing out.

Along with his self-control.

He paused as he walked along the bed of the truck. "Put those in there." He nodded to the easel and stool she held. She laid them in gently and he stepped to the passenger door. "I need you to open the door."

"Why? I'm going home."

"I know." He shifted her in his arms and used the three fingers he freed up to open the door. He slid her onto the seat, being careful not to bump her injured foot. "I'm taking you there. You think that foot is going to be fun to wiggle around while you try to drive?"

Nancy peered down into the floorboard at her ankle. "I ruined my sandal."

"We'll have to get you an actual pair of hiking boots." He pulled out his pocket knife and cut loose a flapping cream colored strap so she didn't risk tripping again. Not that he intended to let her walk anywhere, but with this stubborn woman you could never be too careful.

"We?" Her eyes watched him intently as he started to slip his knife back in the back pocket of his jeans.

Instead of answering he shut her door. The woman didn't miss a damn thing.

He opened his door and slid his bag into the back. Just as he was about to get in, Nancy leaned across the seat, fishing her keys out of her pocket. "I almost forgot. I have candy in my car." She held her keys out. "Could you get it? It's for Easter. For the kids."

He took her keys, letting his hand brush against hers more than he knew was acceptable. Not surprisingly, she didn't seem to mind, letting her hand rest in his open palm.

"Thank you for taking care of me." She smiled.

He nodded and pulled his hand away and went to her car, finding the candy in an embossed paper bag in the back seat. He hooked the twisted paper handles over his wrist and walked back to the truck something about what she said bothered him.

It made him wonder how many times she'd had the opportunity to say it, if ever at all. Had anyone ever really taken care of her? Even as far back as her dad, a man who was never the same after losing his wife, no one that he saw ever took care of her.

He yanked open the door and handed her the candy. She smiled at him and set the bag on her lap.

Maybe someone would have to start taking care of her now.

ELEVEN

PAUL PULLED DOWN Nancy's driveway. This was going to be an interesting experience.

To say the least.

Begging the day off wasn't too difficult. If he was a betting man he'd put money down his boss knew where she could find him.

And was probably happy about it.

He climbed out of his old truck grabbing the plastic bag off the console as he slid off the worn bench seat. Walking to Nancy's door still felt oddly intimidating, even without a protective father waiting for him.

As he stepped onto the porch, the sound of little voices on the other side of the door had him shifting in his boots. More than Jim Dalton ever had when he came to take his oldest daughter out for a date.

It wasn't that he didn't like children, he loved Mina's kids. But Maddie and Charlie were older. They could mostly take care of themselves. He didn't have any experience with the smaller variety and it made him a little nervous, but Beth had to go in to work early this morning for a meeting and Nancy needed help.

And he wanted to be the one to give it to her.

The door flew open just as he was about to ring the bell. Two sets of little brown eyes, lined with thick black lashes and open wide, gazed up at him. Beth's girls were smaller than he expected, but in all honesty he had no idea how big a three-year-old and a five-year-old were supposed to be.

Their mouths hung open as the girls stared silently up at him. He peeked into the house, hoping to see Nancy on her way. The look on their faces was hard to read and the last thing he wanted was two screaming small people.

"Are you a giant?" The little one found her voice first.

"No."

The older girl's eyebrows came together. "Are you sure? Cause you're ginormous."

"Girls?" Nancy's voice called from the kitchen but it took a few seconds before she appeared in the doorway opening to the living room.

She started at the sight of him. "I didn't hear the doorbell."

He smiled at her. It was a nice change to be the one doing the surprising. "I didn't get the chance to ring it."

Nancy cocked her head to one side and raised an eyebrow as she put her hands on her hips. "What have we talked about?" She glared at the girls. "You do not open the door to anyone."

"But you said Mister Paul was coming. We knowed who it was." Liza put her own hands on her hips and matched Nancy's glare.

Paul took a deep breath as he tried to keep from laughing. That little apple didn't fall far from the family tree. It looked like Nancy wasn't the only one who would be bringing some excitement to his day.

Nancy dropped her arms and started gimping to the door in her sock feet, favoring the ankle she sprained. Or the toe she broke. Or both. "It doesn't matter if you know who it is or not. Just because you know someone doesn't mean they are good."

Both girls took a quick step away from him. "Is he good?" They eyed him suspiciously.

Finally making it to the door, Nancy waved him in and closed it at his back. "Yes." She looked up at him, her eyes catching his. "He is good."

Turning back to the girls she clapped her hands together. "Come on, I have breakfast ready." She used one hand on each girl's back to direct them to the kitchen. Turning back over her shoulder she smiled at him.

"Hungry?"

He was starving. He rushed out of the house without so much as a cup of coffee to be sure he had enough time to make a stop on the way. The mention of food and the smell of bacon wafting from the kitchen made his stomach growl in protest.

"A little."

He followed all three girls into the kitchen and set the bag from the drug store he stopped at on the counter before shucking his coat and hanging it over the back of one of the light oak spindle backed chairs at the kitchen table.

Nancy pointed to the cabinetry beside the sink. "Could you grab a couple small plastic cups from that cabinet and fill them halfway with milk?"

Paul did as she asked, pulling one purple and one pink tumbler from the lowest shelf. He eyeballed the cups. They were really small. Half a cupful wouldn't amount to much. He splashed a little more in each one then carried them to the table and set pink in front of Kate and purple in front of Liza. He barely made it back to return the milk to the fridge when he heard a little voice behind him.

"Uh-oh."

He turned to see Liza's cup on its side and a river of milk running across the table to stream over the edge and onto the linoleum floor. She looked at him and wrinkled her nose.

"I made a accident."

Nancy grinned at him as she pulled a well-worn dish towel from the cabinet under the sink. "That's why I only fill them halfway."

Taking the towel from her hands, he went to wipe up the mess. The faucet kicked on and a few seconds later Nancy was at his side, using a wet rag to swipe at the areas he'd sopped most of the milk from. Her side gently bumped against his as she swiped the floor clean.

He stood, holding his hand out to her. Nancy's skin was soft but her grip was firm as she held his hand and pulled up to stand close. Her hand was still clasped tightly in his as she smiled at him.

"Can I have more milk?" Liza's voice drug his attention back to the mess he inadvertently helped create. The little girl held her empty cup out as he wiped up the side and across the top of the table. "Puh-leeze."

He gave her a wink as he took it gently from her hands and went to fill it back up. This time only a quarter of the way.

Nancy tossed the clean-up towels into the sink before grabbing two small plastic princess plates, putting little scoops of fried potatoes and eggs along with one piece of bacon on each. After adding a fork to each one, she handed him the filled plates.

"Thank you Mister Paul." The girls chimed as he set their plates down on the table in front of them.

He grinned at them as they ignored their forks and started grabbing food with sparkly painted fingers. Women of the smaller variety were decidedly easier to handle than their grown counterparts.

At least so far.

He turned to find Nancy holding out a large ceramic plate piled high with everything the girls had plus two homemade buttermilk biscuits. He raised an eyebrow at her.

"Am I the only one who gets biscuits?"

"We can't has biscuits till we eat our other stuff." Liza shoved in half of her piece of bacon as she sat swinging her legs.

Nancy handed him a cup of coffee. "They'll only eat bread if you give them the option."

Paul smiled. "I'm not sure I can blame them there." He nodded her direction. Where's your plate?"

"I'm getting there." She turned to pour herself a cup of coffee and he seized the opportunity. When she swung back to face him, he held two plates of food a little proud he'd managed in time.

Now he got to wink at her. "Go sit down. I'll bring the food."

She smiled, leaning close as she passed him. "You just don't want to be alone with the mess makers."

He followed behind her, balancing a plate in each hand. "You are right there."

Nancy sat down beside Kate. His butt was barely in the chair beside Liza before she side eyed his plate then looked up at him. Something told him his biscuits were in imminent danger around this angelic looking little peanut.

"I ate my bacon. Can I has a biscuit?" Her voice was quiet, her eyes never leaving his plate.

"No you may not." Nancy pointed her fork at Liza's half eaten plate of food. "Eat your eggs. Then we'll talk."

The little girl huffed as she picked up her fork to stab at the pile of eggs on her plate. She looked up. "Is there jelly?"

"If you eat your eggs there can be jelly."

Liza shoved a big bite in her mouth and chewed loudly in his direction. "Nana makes her own jelly from strawberries that grow out there." She pointed a chubby finger at the backyard before shoving another big bite into her mouth. "She says we can pick some soon."

A chunk of egg flew out of her mouth and landed on his shirt.

"Mouth closed Liza." Nancy shook her head and mouthed a 'sorry' at him.

He smiled back at her. A little egg on his shirt was worth getting to listen to little Liza chatter beside him. She kept him entertained for the rest of breakfast and while he helped Nancy get the girls shoes on.

As Kate was swinging her backpack on he remembered the bag on the counter.

He quickly retrieved it and held it out to Nancy. "I got you this. Hopefully it will be more comfortable than trying to get that toe into your shoes."

She eyed him as she cautiously took it from him then peeked inside, a smile spreading across her face. She reached in and pulled out the walking boot he picked up at the drug store on the way in this morning. She started laughing as she opened the packaging.

"I tried to get it in my shoe this morning and it was awful." She propped her butt against the wall and started to pick up her foot.

"Wait." He took the bag from her hand and pulled out an elastic ankle brace. "I got this too. I'm not sure if it will help, but I figured it was worth a shot."

He dropped to his knees and gently picked up her ankle, resting it on his thigh as he ripped open the plastic on the brace. Carefully stretching the beige fabric, he worked it over her sock until it was snugly hugging her heel.

He looked up to find her eyes watching him intently. "Does that feel okay?"

She nodded silently.

He took the boot from her hand and slid her foot into the boxy black canvas shoe. He wrapped the Velcro straps across the top of her foot and set it back on the ground before standing back up. "Try it."

She gingerly took a step. Then another. "Oh my gosh, that's so much better." She touched his arm lightly as she passed back by him. "Thank you."

He watched her as she grabbed her other shoe off the mat by the door and sat on the couch to put it on her uninjured foot. He put his hand over his arm were she'd touched him, rubbing the spot, trying to get the tingling to go away. Who would have thought a simple touch would have such an effect.

But it wasn't a simple touch. It was appreciation. Acknowledgement. And it was something he'd never gotten much of.

She stood up from the couch and looked at the girls. "Ready?"

They bounced around the room. "Yes!"

A few minutes later everyone was all strapped in and heading into town to drop Kate off at kindergarten with Liza singing loudly in the back seat to some song about putting a ring on it. "Do you like Benoncé Mister Paul?"

He looked up in the rearview, then at Nancy. She leaned across the console and rested her hand in the crook of his elbow. "She means Beyoncé."

"That doesn't help clear anything up for me." What in the world was a Beyoncé?

Nancy laughed. "Beyoncé's a singer." She pointed at the stereo. "She sings this song. Liza loves her."

He wasn't so sure he would share Liza's appreciation of Ben... Bey... whatever this woman's name was, but at least it wasn't Cher.

****

Nancy tried to glance at Paul out of the corner of her eye. He seemed to be more relaxed today than he'd ever been before.

When she was around at least.

It made her want more. More kissing, more touching, but she didn't want to push her luck.

Not yet anyway.

For now, just being with him would have to do.

She pointed out the drop off spot and Paul pulled the car up in front of the school. Kate jumped out and Nancy watched as the teachers and aides directed all the car riders into the doors of the school. As soon as her blonde ponytail disappeared, it was time to pull away and keep the line moving.

"Do you need to pick anything up while we're out?" She looked at Paul. He was still craned around watching the kids as they filed into the school.

"Did she make it in?" His brow furrowed as he looked behind them.

Her heart warmed. Paul was a wonderful man. If only he could calm down. Just a little.

"She did and we have to pull away or people are going to start honking."

He looked at her. "You're sure?"

"Yes."

"Is Mister Paul coming with us?" Liza took a break from singing at the top of her lungs.

"He is. We are going to go home and get some things done while Kate is at school." Nancy turned and gave her a smile as Paul pulled away from the curb.

Satisfied, the little girl went back to singing, filling the car with her sweet, and a little out of tune voice for the rest of the trip back. As soon as they were in the driveway and she was unbuckled, her little legs ran as fast as they could to the back yard.

Paul watched as she took off. "Where is she going?"

"I told her we were going to work on the garden this morning. She wants to help." Nancy shrugged at his confused look. "I think she's worried we're going to run out of strawberry jelly."

Paul looked down at the boot he'd brought her this morning and shook his head. "She's the only one who can help. You're out of commission until you can at least get that thing in a regular shoe." He craned his neck, trying to see Liza as she disappeared behind the house. "I'm going to make sure she's okay."

He took off after her leaving Nancy to make her way slowly to the back of the house. By the time she made it there, Paul and Liza were already tromping through the garden making a pile of dead plant stalks.

"What all do you need done?" He shaded his eyes from the morning sun as he watched her finish the walk to the garden.

Navigating the uneven ground was significantly more difficult than the smooth floors inside the house. She couldn't imagine what she would have done if Paul hadn't brought the boot with him this morning. There was no way she could have gotten a shoe on. She'd tried. The pressure on her toes was unbearable and that didn't even address her ankle issue.

"I hate this." She had things to do and this ankle was a huge inconvenience. And not just to her.

"You might want to see the doctor. Make sure everything is where it needs to be." Paul held up his index finger and jogged to the deck. He returned carrying one of her patio chairs. It was missing the cushion since she'd stowed them all in the barn for the winter, but the waffle weave strapping would work just fine.

She sat down and smiled up at him. "What would I do without you?"

He turned away quickly and went back to helping Liza collect last year's producers, but the blush from her praise made it clear to his ears. Unfortunately, she wasn't the only one who noticed.

"Mister Paul. Why is your face all red? Are you tired already?" Liza stopped working and was staring up at him as if he might fall over any second.

"Nope. Just a little warm from the sun."

"Ooooh." She nodded her head slowly then turned to squint in the direction of the sun, then back at him. "Are you firsty?"

Nancy pushed up out of the chair and waddled toward the house. "I'm on it."

She made it all the way to the back door before remembering they'd never actually made it into the house and the door was still locked. With a frustrated groan she headed back off the deck and all the way around the side of the house to unlock the front door.

With a pit stop in the bathroom to pop a couple more pain pills, it took her nearly ten minutes to be back outside with lemonade for her hard workers. By then, Paul found her wheelbarrow parked behind the shed and had it loaded up ready to be dumped.

She handed him his drink and he finished half of it before handing it back to her. Liza was perched in Nancy's abandoned chair nursing her sippy cup as she soaked up the sunshine.

"Where do you want this dumped?"

She pointed to the far end of her yard where she had a large brush pile. "Is over there okay?"

"I can put it wherever you want." He looked at her closely. "What's wrong? Is your foot hurting?"

She sighed. "I just feel bad. I didn't intend for you to do all of this by yourself."

He looked over at Liza. She'd left the chair and was in the middle of the area of the garden they'd been clearing, picking up handfuls of dirt and throwing them in the air, giggling as it rained down over her head. "I have help."

Nancy groaned. "Now I've got to give her a bath before her mamma gets here." That might have actually been part of the little girl's plan. She would sit in the tub until her skin fell off if you let her.

Paul watched her for a minute longer before he turned back to Nancy, his dark eyes serious. "How is Beth?"

Nancy shrugged. "As well as can be expected I guess." She watched as Liza lay down and started rolling. The sound of her giggles carried across the yard. "She'll be okay. She has to be."

"She deserves to be better than okay. She deserves to be happy."

Nancy turned to him. His dark eyes were the color of the sky before a storm. So grey they were almost black. And they were fixed on her. Because he wasn't talking about Beth. Not really.

"She wants to be happy." Her voice came out as a whisper. That was all she had. It felt like a confession. Admitting that she wanted happiness.

Because it meant she didn't already have it.

A tug on her jacket pulled her attention from him. "Nana, I got a little dirty."

She looked down to find Liza's light brown hair littered with dirt and bits of leaves. Her clothes were worse. Luckily, she was in play clothes, but they would still have to go in the washer before they had a chance to stain.

"It's okay honey. Let's go get you cleaned up." She motioned to Paul that she was going inside with Liza. He nodded.

She got Liza into the tub and sat on the toilet, giving her a little time to play. The day was going so well, but she honestly had no idea where to go from here.

Her cards were on the table and now came the hardest part.

Waiting for him to show his hand.

TWELVE

"HOW MANY?" PAUL held one bottle neck in each hand and turned to Hazel.

"You heard me big boy. Three." She held up three fingers, her painted on eyebrows high on her head. "I'm hosting bridge club this week and it sure as heck isn't going to be some boring tea party like last week."

Hazel's newly cut and styled hair looked particularly white in the overhead fluorescent lighting, but even the bright store couldn't hide that her skin was about a shade darker than usual. Or maybe just pinker. Some sort of cosmetic layer left her natural skin unobservable.

Since she found a group of older women in town who played cards each week, Hazel'd been a little more... fancy. Clothes that hadn't seen the light of day in twenty years were being mixed and matched in various and not always complimentary ways. Then there were the shoes.

Paul carefully set the bottles in the shopping cart Hazel had filled with her groceries for the week. They looked amusingly out of place next to the value sized Metamucil. "You think a bunch of old women are going to drink tequila while they play bridge?"

"Not straight." She rolled her eyes at him. "I'm making tequila sunrises. Those women wouldn't do a shot if it was off Cary Grant's navel." She gripped the cart handle and pushed off, shuffling along behind it in a pair of heels that barely peeked from the hem of her powder blue pants, grabbing a bottle of Irish cream as she passed. Hazel caught his eye as she rested it in the basket on top of her purse. "For my coffee."

He shook his head as she sauntered along. "I'm starting to worry about you Hazel."

"Pshh. What's the worst that could happen to me? I'm older than dirt and I've spent my life taking care of an ungrateful daughter and a crabby old man." She grabbed a pack of Oreo's off an end cap and dropped them in the basket. "I want to have fun now."

That was apparent. Since her husband died last year, Hazel was certainly broadening her horizons. "Do these women know what you're planning?"

The last thing he wanted was a Tuesday afternoon emergency call from a whole houseful of old women who needed a designated driver. Especially if they were anything like the woman he was carting around today.

Hazel's red lips broadened into a smile. "The whole damn group RSVP'd because of it." She wiggled her eyebrows at him, obviously proud of herself but also not understanding what he was asking.

Paul began unloading her cart while she wrestled a gossip magazine from the rack beside her and started to thumb through the glossy pages, licking her finger before each flip. "That's great, but how are they getting there? You can't just send them driving home after."

Hazel's brow furrowed and she dropped the magazine onto the belt with the rest of her groceries. "They're doing that Uber thing." She tugged a tissue free of her sweater sleeve and wiped at her nose, removing a smudge of foundation at the same time. "Did you know they'll just pick you up at your house and take you wherever, then come back and get ya?"

He pulled the buggy through for the bagger to refill her cart. "I did know that." He gave her a gentle poke in the ribs. "I'm surprised you did."

Hazel poked him back. "I don't need to know. I've got your handsome ass to drive me around." She paid for the groceries and he helped her into her light coat before offering her his arm and walking to the parking lot.

He helped her into the passenger seat then loaded her bags into the back. As soon as her belt was buckled Hazel fished out a tube of lipstick and flipped down the visor.

Paul climbed in and started the truck, eyeballing her as she reapplied the reddest lipstick he'd ever seen. "What in the world are you doing?"

She rubbed her lips together and popped them open. "I want to go to the hardware store. I want a step ladder with handles." Hazel pushed her tightly curled hair around as she peered into the six square inches of mirror she had to work with. "Plus, rumor has it there's a new owner and he's supposed to look like Mel Gibson."

He didn't know where she got her information but guessed it was from another eighty-year-old who needed to update her bifocal prescription. "I think they oversold you." Paul pulled out of the grocery lot, not excited about having to see Noel or Neil of whatever his name was again. "Why didn't you say this earlier? Now you've got a bunch of groceries in the back."

She waved her hand at him. "They'll be fine. It's not hot and I didn't get anything frozen. Besides, what would I have done then if he wanted me to stay so he could have his wicked way with me? I needed booze for my party."

"Oh my God." Paul propped his elbow on the lip where the window met the truck door and leaned his forehead into his hand. He had so many issues with that statement he didn't know where to start. "I don't even know what to say to that."

Hazel shrugged. "If I get myself a younger man to take care of me, it'll free you up. Maybe find yourself a new lady friend so you can have your own wicked ways." She grinned at him completely unaware of the nerve she hit.

"I'm fine." His voice was short and angry, even to his own ears. He shook his head, feeling like an ass for snapping at her. "I just mean, I don't mind driving you around."

Hazel zipped her purse closed, completely unaffected. "That's good because I have a doctor's appointment next week and I need a ride." She blew him a cherry colored kiss and winked.

He wasn't lying when he said he didn't mind driving her around. It was impossible to stay in a bad mood when the woman was around. "Maybe I should teach you to drive." Paul parked the truck in the closest spot he could find in front of the hardware store. "Just for fun."

Hazel shook her head. "Can't now." She pointed at her eyes, covered in a heavy layer of blue shadow. "Glaucoma."

REGRET

It was probably a good thing. In hindsight, Hazel behind the wheel of a car, even in an empty parking lot, would be a ride his heart might not survive.

By the time he got around to her side, the older woman was already out and adjusting her powder blue slacks. "We need to go shopping Paulie. I wanna get me some of those skinny jeans the ladies are wearing nowadays."

"You want to wear skinny jeans?" The image of Hazel's bird legs in a pair of tight pants would now be burned into his memory forever. Even without actually seeing it. "I'm not sure you'll like them."

She hooked her purse over one arm and started to the storefront. "It's not about liking them. It's about being fashionable. I'm well past due for a makeover."

He pulled the door open and let her slide in first. That was one day he was going to be busy. She could find another chauffer for that fiasco. Doctor's appointments and grocery shopping, he would do. Driving home drunken Miss Daisy's and department store skinny jean shopping? Not gonna happen.

"Well, that's very nice of you, but I'm just fine."

Paul stopped, his ears straining, as Hazel went on toward the back of the store, her hips sashaying as much as she could manage.

"Oh, no thank you. I can manage very well."

Paul darted up another aisle to avoid running into Hazel as she continued sauntering along. He knew that voice.

Well.

And it didn't sound right. Not at all.

By the time Nancy came into view, she was trying to wrestle her hand free from Neil the store owner, a fake smile still plastered on her face. She was propped onto a set of crutches and a large black medical boot was Velcro-ed around her injured foot.

Neil stepped forward as she tried to back up. "I'd be more than happy to take you home. That way your son doesn't have to worry about it." He gave her a slick smile. "The store's empty. I can close it whenever I want." Then the bastard winked an over-tanned eyelid. "It's a perk of being the boss."

Paul walked up behind him, stepping lightly in his boots. The guy wasn't nearly as tall as he looked standing next to Mike the first time they met. Neil was barely five-ten and Paul towered over him enough to see the bald patch starting at the top of his head. He crossed his arms and cleared his throat.

"Store's not empty."

Neil swung around, his nose nearly meeting the middle of Paul's chest. He had to tip his head back to level his glare. "Can I help you Paul?"

"Nope."

"Well, I'll be happy to ring you up before I take Miss Richards home." He smirked and Paul considered ripping his leather lips right off his leather face.

"You're not taking her home." Paul dropped his arms to his sides. "I am."

"You don't get to decide that." Neil snorted. "She doesn't belong to you."

Paul gently tugged Nancy's crutches free and scooped her up. "Doesn't mean she's not mine." He stomped down the aisle, not giving the woman in his arms any options, not that she seemed ready to object. Her eyes were wide and her mouth was hanging open as a blush crept up her face.

"Come on Hazel." He opened the door with his back as he waited. "We're leaving."

The woman made it to the back of the store just in time to witness the whole scene and was busy giving Neil a once over. She scrunched her nose up at him. "Ginny's a liar. This prick doesn't look anything like Mel Gibson."

****

Nancy stared out the windshield trying to ignore the press of Paul's large, and obviously very strong body, against the side of hers. She tried to keep her expectations, her hopes, low when it came to how things would go with him. All she really wanted was to be his friend.

That's what she kept trying to tell herself, and that's what he tried telling her too, but it appeared they had at least one thing in common.

They were both liars.

"You should have slapped that man across his face honey." The woman in the passenger seat patted her leg with a heavily veined hand. "I'm Hazel. Paulie here dated my daughter a few years back."

"Shit." Paul spoke for the first time since they walked out of the hardware store.

Since he walked out of the hardware store anyway.

For the second time in less than a week, Paul did more than sweep Nancy off her feet and that was causing some major shifts within her. Nancy was feeling ways she hadn't felt in...

Too damn long.

And right now the cab of Paul's truck was way too full of angry man and Hazel for her to even begin to figure out what she could do about it.

But she was going to do something.

"Paulie that was the most romantic thing I've ever seen. Like in that movie where Richard Gere carries the girl out of the factory." Hazel sighed and held her hand over her heart. "My Simon couldn't have picked me up if his life depended on it."

Nancy looked down at the tiny woman beside her. She couldn't weigh a hundred pounds soaking wet. "Really?"

Hazel continued to pat Nancy's leg. "Oh sure honey." She leaned in. "Not all men are like the one beside you."

Nancy felt the heat rush back into her chest. She peeked at Paul out of the corner of her eye. "I know that."

Hazel winked at her. "Then you and I will get along just fine." She leaned forward to look across Nancy. "Paulie stop pouting."

Paul looked toward Hazel, his face a mixture of shock and murder. Nancy looked again. Yup. He wanted to kill Hazel.

"I'm not pouting." He threw the truck into park and opened his door. "And this is your stop." Nancy waited while Paul helped get Hazel and the groceries he pulled from the back seat into her two-story. She watched as they had a very animated conversation on her porch.

Then Hazel pinched Paul's ass and grinned at him from her doorway as he stomped back to the truck. Hazel gave her a wave and shut the front door just as Paul slid in beside her.

He barely had time to close his door before Nancy was twisted in her seat, all but climbing on his lap to press her lips on his. She held his face in her hands as she tried to get closer, needing to feel his body against hers. What he did in that hardware store...

Hazel might call it romantic, but it wasn't. It was the hottest, sexiest, manliest thing she'd ever seen in her whole life.

And it was for her.

He saved her. He protected her. He took care of her. But it was more than that.

He said she was his.

And it made her want to jump him. Right here in the front seat of his old pick-up. She didn't even care if Hazel's little lady eyes were glued to the windshield while she did it.

"Paul." She went back to kissing him, wanting to say so much, but wanting to be as close as possible more.

He tried to pull his lips from hers but she held tighter, forcing him to talk around her mouth. "I'm sorry. I shouldn't have done that."

Damn. Why couldn't he just go with this?

She slumped back to her seat. "You didn't mean what you said?"

REGRET

Paul glanced up toward Hazel's house. "Let's get you home." Nancy followed his gaze and sure enough, a pair of eyes peered out from between the curtains.

Nancy smiled and waved. The drapes flipped shut with a jerk. "That woman is something else."

Nancy watched Paul as he drove, his jaw set, eyes never leaving the road. If he didn't want to kiss, he was going to have to talk. Maybe he'd circle back just to shut her up. "Hazel said you dated her daughter."

His already tense jaw started to twitch.

"Did you two date long?" Now that she'd asked it, Nancy realized she really wanted to know the answer. Was Hazel's daughter as much of a spitfire as she was? Was she as tiny of a woman?

Nancy looked down, suddenly feeling very uninteresting and overly sturdy. And not in a good, strong sort of way.

"Couple years." Paul's quiet response distracted her from calculating the number of pounds she would have on a woman of Hazel's size.

It was fifty.

Maybe she didn't want to know any more about this woman. Maybe it would only make her act even more stupid and insecure than she was right now.

"That's good." She looked out the window hoping the can of worms she'd opened would quietly shut itself and never return.

"She's married now." Paul sighed. "She and her mom had a falling out, so I keep an eye on Hazel. Help her out if she needs anything."

Nancy turned back to him, watching. The man was such a contradiction. On the outside he appeared strong and solid. Unyielding even.

But inside was a different story.

She was beginning to discover, inside he was anything but. He was sweet and gentle. Caring and nurturing. But with his odd reactions when it came to her, she was worried he was also something else.

Paul was broken.

Nancy slowly stretched her arm and rested it above his knee. "Thank you. I wasn't sure how I was going to get out of that store."

He nodded.

"You keep showing up to save me." She smiled as a barely perceptible blush spread across his neck and a tiny smile twitched at the corners of his mouth.

As they turned into her driveway, she was about to ask him to stay for lunch when his expression quickly changed. He looked confused.

"Are you expecting someone?" Paul stared out the windshield.

She turned to follow his gaze. A small car with a rental sticker on the bumper was parked in front of the house and a woman was sitting on her porch.

Not just a woman. Carol Dalton was on her porch. Even after all these years, Nancy would know her sister anywhere.

THIRTEEN

NANCY'S BUTT MIGHT as well have been glued to the worn seat of Paul's truck. She was frozen in place by shock, or confusion, or most likely complete and total disbelief.

"Do you know who that is?" Paul squinted out the windshield.

Carol stood up, her lean frame an almost unmistakable mirror image of Nancy's.

His mouth dropped open. "Holy shit."

"Holy shit's right." The immediate shock was gone and quickly replaced by anger.

What in the hell was Carol doing camped on her front porch? After this many years, what was the point in showing up now?

And of all the times in the world to appear, why did it have to be this one?

Paul turned to her. "I'll be back." He started to get out and she grabbed his arm.

"It's okay. I'll go talk to her." She started to open her door to get out. By the time she managed to get herself turned in the seat and wrestle her crutches from the back seat, Paul was right there.

He took her crutches and held out his hand for her to use as support. Once she was on the move, he stayed close by her side as they slowly made their way up the driveway.

"Do you want me to stay?" He kept his voice low enough she would be the only one to hear.

"Yes." If this was the same old Carol on her front porch, she wanted back-up.

Carol watched as they walked toward her but didn't speak until they were at the bottom of the steps.

"Hi Nan."

It was odd. Paul called her Nan all the time and it never bothered her. Actually, she liked it. It was more familiar than if he called her Nancy and if there was one thing she wanted it was for them to be more familiar.

But Carol. That was different.

This was a woman who left her son when he needed her most. A woman who could sleep with her sister's husband for years and act like nothing was going on. A woman who didn't even show up when their dad died. Worse yet, when her own son died.

"Why are you here Carol?" Nancy kept her words short and tried to be as emotionless as she could manage, even as anger made her want to rip the diamond earrings right out of her sister's ears.

Then she wanted to stab them back through again.

To make matters worse, Carol looked pretty good for a woman Nancy thought might be as dead as their shared bedmate. Her hair was colored a rich but light brown and fell in perfectly straight, shiny, well-behaved strands to just below her chin. Her skin was smooth and surprisingly tan, making Nancy wonder just where she'd spent the past few decades.

Carol hesitated. "I came because I heard about Thomas." She licked her lips, barely putting a dent in the perfectly complimentary shade of peach glossing them. "I just wanted to be here for you if you needed me."

Nancy glanced sideways at Paul. His brow was furrowed and he appeared to be as perplexed as she was. "Well, thank you, but Thomas is fine now."

A flash of confusion passed across Carol's face then her expression softened. "Oh, I know he's in a better place. But that can't take away the pain of the loss for you."

The realization of what was going on made Nancy feel sick. Paul's arm snaked around her waist, strong and solid, giving her the strength to push out her next words.

"Carol, Thomas didn't die."

Carol's head bobbed back as her eyes opened wide in shock. "I'm so sorry." She placed a hand on her chest. "I heard your son died."

Nancy shook her head. "No." She swallowed hard. "Your son died."

Nancy expected shock, crying, at the very least confusion but Carol appeared to be none of those things. She looked... blank.

"Carol? Did you hear me?" Nancy glanced at Paul then back at Carol, not really sure what else to say.

Finally Carol blinked. "Yes. Sorry." She stared across the yard. "It never occurred to me it was Rich they meant." She pulled a tissue from her pocket and began dabbing at her eyes as her chin began to quiver. "I guess it should have since you were the only mother he had." She dropped her head and began softly crying, her face in her hands.

Paul's hand squeezed her hip. She looked up at him as he leaned down. "Let's go inside so you can sit and prop that foot up."

She nodded and leaned against him as he all but lifted her up the few wooden stairs to the porch. If the shit wasn't stuck to the fan and slowly flying off in clumps, the gesture would have been enough to get her engines running again. Luckily, it appeared there was no lack of chivalry in the man gently directing her across the deep green planks of the farmhouse's wrap-around porch.

She patted Carol on the back when she reached the porch, the anger from earlier in check. For now. "Let's go inside."

Paul held the screen door as Nancy unlocked the deadbolt. He let Carol follow her in before coming in and shutting the door behind them. Nancy peeled off her jacket and hooked it on the wall beside the door then moved directly to the couch. She needed to sit down.

Actually, what she could really use was a drink, and a nap. Maybe a good roll around with the man carefully hanging his coat by hers. Unfortunately all those things would have to wait. Some probably longer than others.

Nancy stared at their coats, side by side, and tried to process what in the hell was going on.

If Carol truly was back because of the incorrect belief Nancy needed her, would she expect the same now that the tables had turned? If she did, she might be sorely disappointed because Nancy wasn't sure she had it in her.

Paul's hand on her shoulder, snapped her away from the complicated mess of emotions running through her head, and she jumped under his touch.

"Sorry." He knelt by the arm of the couch where she sat and held out his hand. "Here. Take these."

Two blue gel caps sat in his palm. She grabbed the pills and popped them in her mouth. He held out a glass of water and she swallowed them down then set the glass on the table before propping her foot beside it.

Carol was still standing by the front door, looking around, occasionally dabbing at the corners of her eyes with her mangled tissue. She hadn't been in the house in twenty-five years and some things had changed since then. And not just furnishings.

"Why don't you sit down?" Nancy pointed at the couch across from her.

Paul leaned in as Carol walked across the room. "I'm going to the kitchen. Call if you need me."

Nancy touched his cheek, for the first time noticing he'd shaved. The barest bit of stubble colored his skin and the scent of aftershave still lingered. The concern in his eyes was evident.

It made her want to wrap her arms around his neck and tell him how much she appreciated him. How much his being here meant to her. But it would have to wait.

She nodded and watched as he walked away, already missing his reassuring closeness.

Nancy crossed her arms over her chest. The last thing she wanted to deal with right now was her sister. It might seem heartless considering she'd just had to break the news to Carol that her son was dead, but if the woman cared that much about Rich she wouldn't have walked away without a second thought.

In all truth, part of Nancy wanted her to suffer. The way Rich suffered when she left.

Only Carol was an adult. Rich was a child when she disappeared. He was too young to understand why his mommy was gone. Every day he waited for her to come back and every night he'd cried himself to sleep on Nancy's lap when she didn't.

Nancy narrowed her eyes at Carol as she sat down. No. She didn't want her to suffer the same as Rich. She wanted her to suffer more.

Carol shifted on the couch, crossing one leg over the other. Her well cut black slacks met matching ankle boots with a thick, low heel. A fine-threaded tan sweater clung perfectly to her shoulders in an impeccable fit. She folded her hands in her lap. Her eye caught on Nancy's foot propped on the coffee table.

"Is your foot hurt?"

No, she was wearing this medical shoe as a fashion statement. "I sprained my ankle and broke my toe."

"Oh, that's awful." Carol shook her head. "That must make things difficult."

Nancy glanced in the direction of the kitchen. Not so far it hadn't, but mostly because of the man sitting patiently while she tried to figure out what in the hell to say to her sister.

Carol leaned forward. "If it would help you out, I could stay here while your foot heals."

Nancy was shocked. So shocked, she actually started laughing. This whole situation was outrageous. "Did you actually think you could show up and I would welcome you with open arms?"

Carol's eyes shot wide as a hand went over her heart. "I just thought--"

"You thought what? All was forgiven? We were all here eagerly anticipating your return so everything would be complete again?" Nancy shot up from the couch, ignoring the instant pain the movement caused. "You chose to leave. You only thought of yourself and as far as I'm concerned, you can leave again." Nancy's arm shot out, her finger pointing at the door.

Carol blinked quickly and swiped at the corners of her eyes. "I didn't think anything. I just wanted to help, show you I was sorry."

"Yeah?" Nancy cocked an eyebrow. "Well, if you really want to show me you're sorry you can start by apologizing for fucking my husband."

****

Paul jumped up from the kitchen chair. He was doing his best to stay out of what was happening in the next room, but from the sound of it, things were getting very heated, very quickly.

He crept to the doorway. Nancy was standing up yelling, her finger pointed at Carol, who sat on the couch, her eyes as wide as saucers, mouth hanging open. She'd been gone long enough to miss two important developments. First, Nancy was no longer the cautious older sister, unsure of exactly how best to handle her younger sister's bad behavior. Second, Nancy knew her secret.

After a few seconds, Carol seemed to regain her composure. "You found the letters." Her voice was quiet, her face pale.

"I didn't." Nancy spat the words. "Your son did."

"Oh."

"Did you ever think about him? Just once wonder how he was? What you leaving did to him?"

A tear ran down Carol's cheek. She shook her head. "I thought he would be happy with you."

Nancy rubbed her hands over her face, leaving them to rest at her temples. "You expected me to be able to make up for the fact that he didn't have a father and his mother didn't care enough about him to stick around?" She shook her head. "You are a selfish bitch Carol."

Paul moved further into the room. The only other times he'd seen one woman call another a bitch hadn't ended well and he wanted to be close in case this situation was headed that same way.

Surprisingly, Carol nodded. "You're right. I was. I thought he would be better with you. You were always a much better mother than I was." She wiped at her eyes. "I really thought he would be better off with you."

Nancy dropped her hands to her hips. "You just left to go do whatever you wanted and expected me to raise your son and mine. My husband had just died. Did you even consider that?" Nancy stopped and cocked her head as her eyes narrowed.

"Oh my God. That's why you left." The words were quiet, as if she was talking to herself. She dropped to the couch. "You need to leave."

Carol looked surprised. She looked at Paul where he stood just inside the living room door. He crossed his arms and leaned back against the door jam. If she thought he would help her, she had another think coming.

"Okay." Carol stood and crossed to the door. She quietly pulled it open. She turned to look toward Nancy. "I really am sorry."

Nancy didn't acknowledge her sister, instead continuing to stare at the floor until the door clicked quietly closed and Carol's footsteps tapped across the wooden plank porch.

She turned toward the doorway where he stood. Her face was unreadable.

"You okay?" He was waiting for more yelling or tears. Either would have been a reasonable reaction to what she just experienced.

She furrowed her brow. "I don't know."

The sound of her phone ringing made her jump. "Shit." She twisted on the couch, her eyes scanning the room. "I don't know where I left my phone."

He was already halfway across the room, headed to the rack where her purse was hooked under her coat. He yanked both off and quickly dropped her purse on the couch beside her. As she dug around inside it, he took her coat back to the rack and hung it up.

"Oh God, I forgot to call Thomas." She cringed, her eyes slightly squinting as she answered. "Hello."

He didn't want to seem intrusive so he started back toward the kitchen. He made it two steps before she waved her hand, grabbing his attention.

"I'm sorry." She motioned for him to sit on the couch beside her. "It's been a little crazy and I totally forgot."

Her eyes stayed glued to him as he sat down. She giggled. "You're kidding."

"Jerk. I wouldn't go back there anyway." She rolled her eyes at Paul. "No, I'm fine. I'll tell you about it later." She relaxed back into the couch. "I'm still sorry."

Nancy hung up and slid her phone onto the coffee table. "Thomas was supposed to pick me up from the print shop next to the hardware store." She chuckled. "I guess when I wasn't there he went to the hardware store looking for me and Neil was all fired up."

Yeah. He seemed like the kind of guy to find his nards after the fact. "He give Thomas a hard time?"

She shrugged. "Sounds more like it went the other way around." She leaned toward him ever so slightly. "Just so you're aware, none of us are welcome in his store again."

He shrugged. "At least there's some good news for the day."

Nancy sat for a minute then blew out a long breath shaking her head. "I don't even know what to think right now."

"I can imagine."

She leaned back against the couch. "Would you want to watch a movie?"

There was nothing he wanted to do more. All that mattered to him was that Nancy was okay and he would do whatever it took to make sure that happened.

"I would." He grabbed the remote off the table and handed it to her.

Instead of turning the television on, she stood up and started walking in the direction of the kitchen. "I'm going to get something to drink. Do you want anything?"

He stood up and went after her. "I can get it. You go sit back down." That foot was going to take forever to heal if she didn't start taking it easy.

She stopped and turned to him. "I'm not as helpless as it appears." She sighed and started walking again. "At least I hope not."

He laughed. "It's not about being helpless. It's about being injured and I'm positive you are as injured as it appears. I've seen your foot. I was the one who put your toe back where it belonged, remember?"

She opened a cabinet and pulled out a bottle of wine. "The doctor said as long as I'm careful it will be good as new in a few weeks." She pulled out a glass and held it up, raising her eyebrow in question.

"I don't drink."

"Really?" She eyed him. "When did that happen?"

He took a deep breath and hoped she wouldn't connect the dots. "Few months ago."

Nancy watched him, her expression thoughtful. "After Rich died?"

The woman was too perceptive for her own damn good. At least for his anyway. "Yeah."

She pointed her finger up and down his mid-section. "That why you lost so much weight?"

Paul's hand went to his stomach. It was smaller than when he spent his evenings in the bar, but he was a long way from what he once was.

"I lost a little I guess." He watched as she poured her glass half-full, wondering if she would realize Rich death wasn't just the timing of his sobriety, but also the reason for it. Seeing the damage alcohol could do to innocent people, especially Nancy, it changed him.

She smiled. "Do you feel better? Lighter?"

He didn't, not at first. The weight of his spare tire was nothing compared to the weight of loneliness he'd been drowning around for years. But now... "It's easier to get up a ladder than it used to be."

Nancy took a sip of her wine, watching him as she did. She put her glass down on the counter. "Paul, I'm..." She stopped and looked down at the bits of foil she'd peeled from the neck of the bottle littering the counter. Gently, she used her fingers to dust them into a pile. She stared at the pile of gold shards for a second, then looked up at him.

"I have so many things I want to say to you, but I don't know where to start."

He swallowed hard. "I—"

"I don't want to be alone Paul." Her words tumbled out in a rush. "I never did."

"There've been enough men in town chasing after you. There was no reason for you to be alone." He hated saying it, pointing out how many other men wanted her, talked about having her. He'd been in more than one fight over the years with some asshole who made a rude comment about her.

"I didn't want them." She walked to stand in front of him. "I've been waiting so long for you to forgive me, hoping that maybe one day we could be together, but I don't want to wait anymore." Her voice quivered. "It's too hard. I'm too tired." She shut her eyes and took a deep breath. When she opened them, she seemed more collected.

"Did you mean what you said? About me being yours?" She licked her lips, biting the bottom one for just a second before whispering, "I just need to know."

He stood, frozen. She'd left him two options. Tell her the truth and risk everything, or lie and walk away from her forever, like a coward.

"Please tell me you did." She stepped closer, her clear blue eyes pleading with his as much as her words. "I need you."

Those three words broke him. Broke his resolve. Broke his control. Broke his heart. He wrapped his arms around her waist and pulled her to him, holding her body tightly against his as his mouth covered hers.

He might live to regret this, but he would do anything the woman in his arms needed. Even if that meant risking his own heart. Again.

FOURTEEN

"HOW MANY?" AUTUMN'S green eyes bulged out of her face as she looked up from the notepad sitting on the table in front of her.

"I would plant at least five rows." She paused as a parade of screaming children ran through the kitchen and did a lap around the table. As their giggles and squalls faded into the living room she did mental math. "Yeah. And with those boys it still might not get you all the way through the winter."

Autumn nodded her head as she added the beans to her diagram. "Do you know how many times a day I feed those things?" She finished drawing the long rectangles and labeled them 'beans' then looked back up at Nancy. "Like, six. And I don't mean little snacks. I mean like, meals."

"That sounds believable. I couldn't keep the boys full sometimes." Nancy leaned in to look at Autumn's garden plan. "What about cucumbers?" Nancy turned in the squeaky wooden kitchen chair trying to orient herself. She pointed to the far side of the house. "Most of the sun is on that end, right?"

Autumn chewed her lip for a minute. "It shouldn't be this hard to remember which side of the house is the sunny one."

"You only have so much brain capacity and kids fry half of it." Nancy crossed the kitchen to peer out into the drizzly day. "If it weren't so crappy outside we'd be able to tell." She shrugged Autumn's direction. "It doesn't really matter this instant. We'll figure it out before it's time to put anything in the ground."

"Boys!" Autumn jumped up from her chair and hurried through the living room door. She stopped, looking a little stunned. She turned back to the kitchen and sat down. "It was too quiet, but they're sitting on the couch with the girls watching an episode of something with princesses and unicorns."

With the rain, today ended up being the perfect day to spend with Autumn and her boys. The kids all got to play and burn off steam, while the two women worked out a plan for Autumn's garden.

"Thank you so much for helping me do this. I'm so excited." Autumn carefully tore off her garden map and stuck it under an

Urgent Care magnet on the fridge. "Jerry is making me a little greenhouse for outside to start my seeds in."

Nancy peeked in at the kids. All five of them were sitting in a quiet row on the large sectional, staring at the television. "I'm a little jealous. I've always wanted one of those." Nancy turned her head to grin at Autumn. "Maybe a big one though."

Autumn raised her eyebrows. "I would think it wouldn't be too hard to convince a certain someone to make you something like that." She snorted. "Heck, he'd probably run you a whole irrigation system and electricity."

Nancy gave the kids one last glace before going back to sit beside Autumn. She'd been dying to talk to someone about everything that was happening and poor Autumn was her only option. Not that she imagined her friend would mind one bit.

"Can I tell you something?"

Autumn nodded excitedly, her hair bobbing in time with her head. "Tell me everything."

Nancy leaned in. "So I went to the hardware store downtown..."

Her insides were full of butterflies at the memory of Paul sweeping in and sweeping her out. Hazel was right. It was like a scene in a movie.

Autumn started giggling.

"What?" Nancy straightened a little.

Autumn scrunched her face up as another giggle escaped. "I already know about this."

Nancy sat all the way up. "How do you know?"

"I think everyone in town knows." Autumn looked at her apologetically. "If it makes you feel any better there are a lot of women who are super jealous of you."

Nancy tried to seem casual but it was nearly impossible. "They should be. It was so..." She tried to find a word that a grown up woman would use to describe what Paul did.

Autumn came up with one first. "Fucking hot?" Her voice was low and she scooted her body down to match it, immediately looking over her shoulder to be sure no little ears were near.

Nancy looked too, then back again when the coast was clear. "It was so hot. Holy cow." She shook her head still a little in disbelief over the whole thing.

"So are you guys a thing now?" Autumn was on the edge of her seat, fingers resting on her chin in anticipation.

Nancy sighed. "It seems like it, but—"

"No buts." Autumn shook her head. "None. Just be happy."

"Can I tell you something and have it stay just between us for now?" There was more Nancy needed to talk to someone about but she needed to be sure it went nowhere until she knew how best to handle it.

Autumn's whole face changed. Her expression grew serious. "Of course." She studied Nancy for a minute, her green eyes intense. "Is everything okay?"

In all honesty she didn't know. If her sister was still the same old Carol, she was a loose cannon. Always had been. Her moods were impossible to predict and even harder to deal with.

"My sister Carol's back."

Autumn looked completely and utterly befuddled. It was probably the same way Nancy looked when she saw the woman on her front porch after all these years. Her mouth dropped and her forehead wrinkled as her brows came together. "She's not dead?"

Nancy shook her head. "Is it bad that I thought the same thing when I saw her? I was shocked she wasn't dead." Even worse, on more than one occasion in the few days since, Nancy wished she was.

It would just be so much easier.

"I just can't believe it." Autumn stood up and opened her fridge. "You want a drink?"

"Sure." Nancy crossed her arms and leaned against the back of the chair. "I really can't believe it either." She flung her arms out. "And why now? I was just—"

"You were just about to start enjoying fun time with Paul." Autumn turned from the counter with a tumbler in each hand. She set one in front of Nancy. "And now you've got to deal with her dumb ass."

Nancy took a gulp of the fruity iced tea, then set the glass back on the table, spinning it with her fingers. "It just sucks."

"What sucks?"

Of course she would teach Liza a new word. Like the kid needed to know any more.

"What's a matter?" Liza sprawled onto the tile floor at Nancy's feet, looking up at her. "You look pissed."

Nancy shook her head. "Honey, that's not a nice word."

The little girl used one foot to start scooting her body across the floor, causing static to collect in her hair, pushing the strands to cling across her face. She swiped at them and used her tongue to spit them out of her mouth. "But I like it."

Autumn snorted and tried to turn a laugh into a cough, turning her back to them.

Nancy thought for a minute, her overworked mind making it a struggle. There had to be some argument there somewhere, but right now pissed was a pretty accurate description of how she was feeling about the whole Carol situation. However, it didn't sound right coming out of a sweet little three-year-old's mouth. Funny, just not right.

"Well honey, I like it too, but…" She leaned forward and tickled Liza's belly where it was sticking out of her shirt. "It just doesn't sound very lady like."

Liza squirmed under her fingers as she wiggled them on her chubby little stomach. "I don't wanna be a lady." She grabbed at the hem of her shirt and tugged it down as far as she could manage.

Nancy stopped tickling and sat back up, giving Liza a firm look. "You don't have to be a lady, but you do have to act like one."

The little girl groaned as she sat up. "Does Kate have to be a lady too?"

"Yes." Nancy nodded.

Liza stood up and stomped to the living room, yelling at her sister. "Kate, Nana says you gotta act like a lady."

Autumn shook her head as Liza continued to holler at the other kids, the group finding a second wind of activity. "I think boys are easier." She stared across the room for a second, then turned to Nancy.

"You think Carol knows about them?"

That hadn't occurred to her.

"I don't know."

It didn't matter. Nancy would die before she'd let Carol close enough to those girls to hurt them the way she hurt their daddy.

****

"What in the world is that?"

Hazel looked down, then back at him. "What?"

If she didn't understand his problem with her outfit then there was no sense explaining it to her. He shook his head and held open the front door. "Never mind."

Hazel's keys jangled along with an extra-large stack of bangle bracelets lined up her thin arm. She pulled the door shut and shoved her key in, twisting it in the lock before wrestling it back out again. "You just don't understand the trends. This is what all the girls are wearing this spring."

She dropped her keys into her snake skin print bag and grabbed his arm as she started down the stairs, teetering in a pair of thick-heeled open-toe boots.

They were the biggest oxymoron he'd ever seen. Who in the hell thought to make boots with no toes? "Where did you get those?"

Hazel tugged up her pants leg and twisted her foot from side to side. "Can you believe Ginny's granddaughter was gonna get rid of these?"

He could.

Hazel pulled out the draping top of the black jumpsuit hanging from her tiny frame. "This too."

Paul opened the passenger door of his truck. "No accounting for taste."

Hazel stepped on the side rail and scooted into place. "Her loss." She set the snake purse on the seat beside her. "Doesn't it look good with my cardigan?"

Good was not the word he would use. The sweater did match the cream colored turtleneck she wore under the whole getup. "Uh-huh."

He started to close the door. "Watch your toes." Those shoes weren't going to protect them, that's for sure.

He settled in behind the steering wheel and started driving in the direction of Hazel's doctor's office. "How was bridge?"

"It was fine." She turned in her seat as much as the seatbelt across her chest would allow. "How is that Nancy?" Hazel wiggled her eyebrows. "She's a pretty girl."

"Yup." They were barely off Hazel's street and she was already starting in on him. It was going to be a long, ten minute drive.

Hazel sighed loudly and folded her hands in her lap. "I'm glad the two of you are finally coming together."

"What do you mean by that?"

"Oh Paulie, calm down." She patted his arm. "When you and Sharon broke up..." Hazel's voice trailed off and her eyes lost focus. The older woman swallowed hard before continuing. "Before we quit talking, she told me how you were still in love with a girl from school."

Paul's heart ached for Hazel. He knew she missed her daughter more than she let on. If he thought it would do any good, he'd call Sharon himself, but chances were she'd hang up on him before he got two words out.

"It's better for you to be with a woman who appreciates the good people in her life anyway." Hazel reached over and patted his leg.

Paul glanced her direction. "I don't think she'd agree that I'm good people."

Hazel threw her hands up, the silver bangles rattling as she did. "That's my point. That girl wouldn't know a good man if he picked her up and carried her away." Hazel gave him a grin. "But it seems like Nancy sure does." She wiggled her eyebrows at him.

"I don't think it was as big of a deal as you think it was." He just wanted to get Nancy out of that store before he went for plan B and knocked Neil's veneers out.

"Oh, Paulie." Hazel adjusted the fabric sweeping across her chest, pulling it closed in the middle, only to have it fall open again. "You don't understand how women think. The bridge ladies all went nuts."

He should have known when he caught her peeping through the curtains that the woman wouldn't be able to keep her mouth shut. "What do you mean the bridge ladies went nuts?"

"Well of course I told them." She rolled her eyes at him. "It was the most exciting thing to happen to me in years." She waved her hand between them. "Besides, you should be proud. You got a group of old ladies all hot and bothered and if you can do that, you can do anything."

"Hazel, I've seen you get hot and bothered over a cologne commercial." He parked the truck and went to help her out. She was talking before he opened the door.

"Why is it so hard for you to imagine you might be a good catch?" She poked him in the chest. "And by might, I mean you are." She poked him again. "How many men take care of an old lady whose daughter they used to date?"

He held his hand out, hoping she would take it and stop jabbing his sternum. "I don't know."

She grabbed his hand. "I do. None." The synthetic fabric of her get-up offered no friction against the worn cloth seat and she slipped right down. Her boots hit the pavement and her knees started to buckle from the impact. Paul grabbed her waist to keep her from ending up a pile of rayon and cabled cardigan on the blacktop.

She grabbed his shoulders and let out a yelp, trying to get her feet back under her. He held her steady until she grinned up at him. "Maybe you should carry me in."

He let go of her waist and cocked his head to one side. "You did that on purpose."

She slung her purse over her arm and looked at him over one shoulder as she sauntered away. "Prove it."

Paul shut the passenger door and followed Hazel inside. By the time he made it in, she was already at the receptionist's desk giving them her name. "While I'm here I want to talk to her about that Botox too."

Good God. He shook his head and went to sit down while she finished checking in. She was still at the desk, chatting with the woman when a male nurse opened the waiting room door and called her name.

"Oh honey." She strutted as well as one could expect a seventy-five-year-old woman to strut in heels, in the man's direction, batting her eyes. "I haven't heard a man call my name in years."

The nurse looked in Paul's direction. Paul gave him a smile and a nod. For a few minutes at least, she was his problem.

Paul grabbed a Men's Health from the table beside him. Some shirtless actor half his age was on the cover, his chiseled abs greased up to a high gloss sheen.

There was a time he could have given the guy a run for his money. Of course that time was before he developed a taste for beer and bad food. Giving up one of those vices knocked off an easy forty pounds, bringing him to within twenty of his high school days.

There was one person he knew who still looked exactly like they did in high school. Same lean, strong body with softness in just the right places. It was obvious just by looking at her, but now he'd done more than look at her and he knew for sure.

REGRET

Nancy Richards was still just as hot as she'd always been.

Paul looked down at his still soft stomach. And he'd let himself go.

Sure he'd made some progress, but not enough. Not nearly enough. Especially since there was one thing he couldn't give her. One very important thing.

And he had to find a way to make up for it.

FIFTEEN

WHAT IN THE hell was he thinking?

This seemed like a great idea twenty minutes ago but now it felt more like certain death. A quickly approaching and excruciatingly painful one at that.

Paul bent at the waist, hands on knees, intending to suck air into his screaming lungs. Unfortunately, the new position was only encouraging the limited contents of his stomach to crawl out of their home.

He stood up and started running again. He couldn't breathe and his legs were on fire, but the risk of chucking in the middle of the sidewalk was greatly reduced and that was what counted.

REGRET

All he was trying to do was find a way to sort out all the crazy shit going on in his life. The kind that kept you up thinking at night.

That was a lie. If it meant he had Nancy, he could field any insanity that came his way.

No, it was actually the sudden, unrealistic urge to be what he once was that drove him to make this very, very bad decision. One he was regretting more and more with each passing second and each painful step.

It was Saturday morning for Christ's sake. The first comfortably warm one this spring and this is how he decided to spend it?

Tying up his shoes it sounded simple enough. Go out, zip around downtown, then come home and be one step closer to having the body of his younger self.

He'd lost his fucking mind, foolishly thinking between his forty pound weight loss and working a pretty physical job this would be a piece of cake. Dumbass.

Now, instead of just his legs, his whole body was on fire. He felt like puking, even without bending over. His lungs seized up half a mile ago leaving him wheezing like an asthmatic.

What in the hell was wrong with Mina? She did this every freaking day. Acted like it was the greatest thing ever. Helped her get through the toughest times of her life she said.

Maybe it was because anything seemed easy compared to this stupidity.

Paul rounded the corner near the firehouse and there he saw it. Like a gift from heaven, a bench was less than twenty feet away. He stumbled up to it, his feet resisting any semblance of actual steps now, and sat on one edge falling backwards onto the seat. Draping his arm over his face to block the sun, Paul forced his breathing to slow and swallowed the saliva accumulating in his mouth in an attempt to keep the contents of his stomach firmly in place.

He was a good mile and a half from his house. That meant no matter how he felt, his old ass had to get back up again. Unless he stroked out right here on the bench.

There had to be some other, less horrifying way to tighten up the places that loosened while he wasn't paying attention. He'd have to find it if he was serious about this getting back in shape thing, and he was almost sure he was. Less sure than he was the first few steps out his door this morning, but still pretty sure.

Nancy aged really, really well. Much better than him and that was a problem, mostly for his ego, but also in another way. The more he saw of her the more wanted to see, but as exciting as it was to imagine her body looking as good as it felt, it only brought attention to his other, much bigger, problem.

His dick didn't work.

At least not the last couple times he tried to put it to use anyway.

"Shit." Paul twisted, trying to get more comfortable. The hard wood slats of the bench were digging into his shoulder blades through the sweatshirt he threw on, making the flesh around them hurt. Giving up, he pulled himself into a sitting position and pushed his head between his knees.

After a few more minutes, the urge to vomit and the threat of passing out from lack of oxygen began to subside. Unfortunately without the discomfort to distract him, he now had plenty of brain capacity to focus on what he was only just now willing to acknowledge. Mostly because he never truly believed this thing with Nancy would ever make it this far.

What woman wanted a man who couldn't fuck her? Sure, there was more than one way to skin a cat. There was no doubt in his mind he could please her other ways, but it wasn't the same. It wasn't for a man, and he could only assume it wasn't for a woman either.

"Hi Paul."

He jerked up straight. The sudden movement made him dizzy and brought back the nausea. Or it was something else making him sick to his stomach.

Carol stood close in front of him, smiling brightly.

Paul squinted up at her. He remembered Nancy's younger sister from high school but still probably wouldn't have recognized her yesterday if she and Nancy didn't look so much alike. Carol wore too much make-up and her hair was a weird color, plus he was fairly certain she had some of that paralyzing stuff Hazel was so keen on in her face, but otherwise, they could almost be twins.

He gave her a nod. "Carol."

There was nothing good he had to say to the woman so it was best to keep it short. Since he was still not caught up on his oxygen intake it was easy to do.

"I'm glad I ran into you." She sat down beside him clearly unaware he didn't have any intentions of conversing with her. "Can you think of any way I could smooth things over with Nancy?" She crossed one leg over the other and leaned ever so slightly toward him. "I just don't know how I can show her how sorry I am."

He considered suggesting she just leave. Considering her past behavior it wasn't too far out of the realm of possibilities. Unfortunately, it looked like she was planning on staying around, at least for now.

Carol scooted even closer. She blinked long and slow at him and when she spoke again her voice was low and soft. "I mean, how was she able to get you to forgive her for what she did to you?"

This was uncharted territory for him. Up until now, anyone who he considered a threat to Nancy had a sack between their legs. If they got out of line, he'd gently put them back where they belonged. Usually with his fists. But that option was off the table in this scenario.

"Just leave her alone." He scooted down the bench needing a little more distance from the woman whose mere presence threatened the happiness of the person who meant more to him than anyone in the world.

"Oh Paul!" Carols eyes quickly filled with tears. "I never realized how deeply I hurt her." She flung her arms out as she leaned his direction.

He slid off the edge of the bench, narrowly avoiding her body as she attempted to collapse against him. She caught herself and looked up at him, crocodile tears running down her cheeks.

Paul stepped back, making sure he was far outside her reach. He wasn't ever going to be her shoulder to cry on. "I'm sure you'll figure something out."

He immediately turned and took back off in a decent jog, anger propelling him forward as he pushed himself to put as much distance between them as possible. That woman had some nerve trying to put him in the middle of her mess. If she thought he would ever put the trust Nancy had in him on the line to help her, well she would be dead wrong.

Before he knew it, his legs were carrying him up the steps to his front porch. He was back at home. Not too awfully sick feeling or even too terribly tired. Breathing a little heavy, but in a good way.

Maybe Mina was on to something after all. It just took the right emotion to get moving. In his case, anger.

Letting himself in, Paul grabbed a bottle of water from the fridge and stood in the middle of the room, tapping one foot as he sipped.

He felt better than he had this morning when he finally gave up on sleeping and drug his exhausted ass out of bed. The feeling of being ready to crawl out of his skin as he pulled out every hair in his head was all but gone. He pulled out a chair at the table and sat down, stretching his legs out in front and leaning back.

He'd tossed and turned all night trying to figure out what in the hell his problem was. For years, he'd stayed away from Nancy, always for the most noble sounding reasons. Her husband died. She was busy raising two boys. She had a business to run. Most recently, Rich died.

The reasons always sounded right and respectful and honorable, but deep down, they were all one thing and one thing only.

Lies.

He didn't stay away from Nancy for her. He stayed away from Nancy for himself. He made every excuse he could think of to stay away from her. All for one reason.

He was a chicken shit.

A scaredy cat.

A pussy.

Deep down, he never blamed Nancy for choosing Sam, because deep down he always thought Sam was better. At least until he found out the kind of husband Sam had really been to her. He'd been a shitty friend, but it never really occurred to Paul he would be just as shitty of a husband.

But even once he found out just what Sam was, he still didn't pursue Nancy. He made a million excuses why, but the real reason was one he never could admit to.

Now he was faced with all those excuses being shot down. And he still was grasping at straws, trying to find some bullshit reason to step away from the only woman he'd ever really wanted.

What the fuck was wrong with him? Even as she told him she wanted him, needed him, all he could do was try to think of reasons she shouldn't. Try to think of reasons to leave her alone, and he couldn't figure out why.

Until this morning anyway. As he was panting his way down the sidewalk, wondering what in the hell he was thinking deciding to just up and take off for a run, he realized exactly what he was doing.

He was still trying to make himself good enough for her.

****

"You are shitting me."

Nancy leaned her face into her hands. "You have no idea how much I wish I was."

"Son of a bitch." Thomas leaned back in his chair and crossed his arms over his chest. "Did she leave?"

"I don't know." She hoped so. It was awful to say, but there was no reason for her to stay. The only reason Nancy would have ever hoped for Carol's return was gone now, a victim of his mother's selfish decisions.

"Does she have any idea what she did to Rich?"

"I don't know." Carol had never really been one to think of how her actions might affect other people. Obviously.

Nancy always assumed it was due to the fact they lost their mother at a young age. Jim did his best, but his own grief kept him from being there the way two young girls needed. Carol ended up so focused on her own feelings of loss and sadness that she never learned to think about anyone else's emotions, even her own son's. As a result, she put Rich through exactly what she experienced as a child.

Worse actually. Their mother didn't choose to leave them. Cancer made the decision for her.

"Are you going to tell Beth?"

Thomas had so many questions and Nancy had no answers for him. "I think that's something we need to talk about."

"She needs to know." Mina looked up from across the table.

Thank God. Nancy was beginning to worry that the person whose opinion she really wanted was not going to offer it up. Mina had been quiet for the entire conversation. Probably as shocked by the whole thing as Nancy was.

Mina leaned onto the table. "You can't shelter her. She's strong. She needs to know."

Nancy could feel her emotions tightening her throat. "I just worry it will do more harm than good." Beth appeared to be doing better, coming out of the dark place she was in after Rich's death and Carol showing up could derail her progress.

It sure as hell was screwing up Nancy's.

"I don't think so." Mina looked at Nancy across the table. "It's difficult to be angry at someone who's dead. Even if they deserve it."

Boy, didn't she know that. If Rich was still alive she would want to kick his ass. But he wasn't. He was dead. Coming to terms with that was the easy part. Dealing with who he was at the end was...

Mina shrugged. "It might actually help her to have someone to direct her anger at. Even if she never sees her face to face, just being able to feel angry with no guilty strings attached might help her move in the right direction."

It was all so overwhelming. Nancy tipped her head back and tried to relax as tension started to build in her shoulders. "I don't know how to tell her."

"I know, but it has to come from you." Mina reached across the table to grab her hand. "I don't know if you realize how important you are to Beth, especially right now."

Nancy shook her head. "I know I help her out with the girls, but she and her mother are so close."

Mina squeezed her hand. "That's all well and good, but her mother has never been through anything like what Beth is going through right now." Mina leaned closer, her eyes serious. "You are the only person who has lost exactly what Beth has lost. She needs you."

Nancy propped her elbows on the table and held her head in her hands, using the fingertips of each hand to massage her temples. This was not something she was equipped to deal with, let alone help someone else deal with. "I don't know that I can be any help to her."

At this point Nancy didn't know how she felt about Carol's sudden reappearance. Part of her was angry. Part of her was confused.

Part of her was suspicious.

Why in the hell did she just show up after all these years? She said it was because she thought Nancy needed her, but Carol was never one to want to help anyone.

At least not the Carol who left her son in her sister's care and skipped town.

Nancy sat up straight. She was going to have to tackle this situation head on. "I think I need to talk to Carol before I tell Beth."

Beth was as much her daughter as Rich was her son, and Nancy would be damned if she risked her well-being simply because she didn't want to deal with her difficult sister. "Maybe she won't be as big of a pain in the ass as she was thirty years ago."

One could only hope.

"I wish there was something I could do to help." Mina's brow was furrowed with concern.

Thomas straightened. "I'll go with you."

Nancy patted his arm. "No. I'll be fine."

Now that she thought about it, talking to Carol might make her better than fine. There was a lot Nancy wanted to say to her. For herself, for Beth and the girls.

For Rich.

"I have a lot to say to your aunt Carol. There's some things she and I need to get straight if the woman wants to have a snowball's chance to meet Beth." It was time for Carol to understand exactly what she did when she left all those years ago. To realize how her decision affected people then, and continued to cause pain for people now. Of course this all hinged on one thing her sister wasn't known for.

Being willing to listen to someone's mouth besides her own.

SIXTEEN

PAUL GROANED AS he forced his aching body out of the truck. As miserable as he felt yesterday during his run, it was nothing compared to the agony he was in today. Every muscle in his body screamed in protest of any move he made.

He took the hottest shower he could stand hoping it would help, and it did, for all of five minutes. Now, after sitting in his truck the mere fifteen minutes it took to get to Nancy's, his body was already tightened back up. Lifting his feet from the ground was nearly impossible, forcing him to shuffle along like an eighty-year-old man.

The door swung open. Paul tried to straighten up and walk like a normal human instead of the missing link, but it quickly became obvious his attempts were ineffective. The concern furrowing Nancy's brow was visible even from twenty feet away and it only became worse the closer he came.

"Are you okay? Why are you walking like that?" She stepped to the side letting him walk inside before closing the door.

He stopped, needing to rest just a minute and give the muscles twitching in the back of his legs a chance to calm down. "I'm fine, just a little stiff."

He felt her hands gently tug at the shoulders of his jacket, slipping it down his arms. If it hadn't been such a struggle to get it on, he might have put up a fight over her babying him. How in the hell his arms and shoulders ended up just as sore as his legs, he'd never know. Unfortunately, he wasn't so sure he could get the damn thing off himself so he let her take it and hang it up.

"Are you hurt?" She ran her hands over him, slowly.

He wanted to explain, but the feel of her hands as they softly ran across his back to his shoulders and down his arms was such a welcome distraction to the self-inflicted discomfort he'd been suffering from made it hard to focus on anything else besides the feel of her touching him.

Suddenly she stopped. Paul's eyes flew open. He hadn't even realized he'd closed them. She was standing in front of him, her brow furrowed and a frown on her face.

"What's wrong?"

She raised an eyebrow. "I've been asking you the same thing."

REGRET

He cleared his throat as he tried to clear his mind and refocus. "I went for a run and I'm a little sore."

"A run." She crossed her arms over her chest. "What possessed you to go on a run?"

He mentally tossed around different explanations he could give and tried to come up with the least embarrassing yet still plausible option.

"Osteoporosis." He read an article that people who partook in regular weight bearing exercise were less likely to suffer from osteoporosis. While he wasn't old by any stretch of the imagination, it wasn't as far off as it was twenty years ago.

Nancy smiled, her lips were smooth and satiny looking as they separated to expose her teeth. All perfectly aligned, with the exception of a small gap between her front teeth that he would argue was also perfect.

"I don't know that osteoporosis is something you should be worrying about."

"I could say it is something everyone should be worried about." He eyed her trying to gauge if she believed his excuse. He'd hoped to be able to simply tighten some things up without anyone, most importantly Nancy, noticing. Especially since his reasoning was rooted in insecurity.

"Fair enough." She took a step toward the kitchen. "Hungry?"

She would quickly discover that was a question where he would never answer no. When it came to good food, he was always hungry. "I am."

He was quickly becoming spoiled. In the past week he hadn't eaten cold bologna once. He spent almost every night with Nancy and she cooked each one of them, sending him home with any leftovers.

Paul followed Nancy into the kitchen, the smell of dinner making his empty stomach growl. He'd skipped lunch just in case and now he was beyond starving.

Man was he glad he did.

Nancy made chili with homemade cornbread. The chili had chunks of meat mixed in with the normal ground beef and two types of beans. The cornbread had cheese and jalapenos making it rich and spicy and the perfect accompaniment to the chili.

He ate more than he should have, but it was hard to stop. Just like everything else was with Nancy. Hard to stop once he started.

Nancy smiled across the table at him as she finished the last spoonful of her dinner. "Good?"

"Very." He resisted the urge to rub his stomach, instead leaning back against the chair.

"See what you missed out on by not getting married?" Her eyes were glued to him as the words left her mouth.

He could tell her that's not why he never got married. He could tell her she was the only woman he'd ever imagined himself marrying. But he wouldn't. Not yet anyway.

So, he just smiled and stood up, stacking her bowl in his and taking them to the sink. As he ran the water, she came behind him, hooking one finger in the belt loop on the side of his jeans.

"You can leave those." She leaned into his side, her breast rubbing across the outside of his bicep. "We can watch a movie." She looked up at him, her eyes holding his as she shifted her weight allowing her breast to drag back across him. The pale blue of her eyes filled with the blackness of her pupils as they dilated. Her lips parted and a barely perceptible flush tinted her skin.

It was a look he'd imagined seeing on her face many times over the years but now only struck fear deep inside him. Nancy wanted him and the realization was enough to make him consider another run. One that would be straight to the driver's seat of his truck.

Because as much as he might want to take her in every way she wanted him to, based on recent history, the chances of that being possible were slim.

He shut off the water and followed along as she gently led him, her index finger still caught on the waistband of his jeans. He tried to stay calm as she sat down and tugged him down beside her.

Over the past few weeks he tried convincing himself she might not even be interested in this sort of thing. Maybe she just wanted companionship and company. Both things he was more than capable of giving her.

But every moment they spent together brought more subtle hints that was not the case and tonight it appeared she was done being subtle. The reality was this was going to happen eventually and sooner was better. That way, it wouldn't hurt so much when she rejected him.

"You look pale." Her eyes widened as she studied his face. She scooted away from him. "I didn't mean to…" She folded her hands in her lap. "Please don't leave. I'll keep my hands right here. I promise."

Holy shit. It never occurred to him that as much as he was picking up on her signals, she was also picking up on his. And obviously he was coming across loud and clear.

How in the fuck did he end up here? He was a man for Christ's sake. He was supposed to be the one who promised to keep his hands to himself. He was the one who was supposed to be doing the chasing, the touching, the seducing. Oh God.

He was the woman.

He sat up straight. No fucking way could this go on. Nancy needed a man. She wanted a man. She deserved a man. And last time he checked, he was a man, even if the dick between his legs was unreliable at best.

He leaned across the couch and caught her around the waist, running his hand up the middle of her back to tangle in her hair as he used his knee for leverage, ignoring the pain the movement caused. He drug her under him, pressing her into the couch as he caught his weight on his arms.

He didn't kiss her right away. Instead he let himself enjoy everything about these first few seconds. The first few seconds of things being what they should have from the beginning. The feel of her body under his, her hands gripping his shoulders, her hair between his fingers, her scent, her breath, her eyes on his.

He waited as long as he could, until not feeling her lips under his became almost painful. Slowly, he leaned down. Her eyes fluttered closed, her lashes dark against the pink flush of her cheeks. A flush that was there because of him.

He gently brushed his lips across hers, keeping his eyes open, wanting, needing to watch her every second. He pressed harder. Her lips parted immediately. He loved the taste of her. He tipped his head taking the kiss deeper.

She sighed into his mouth as her body relaxed under his. Her hands went to fork into his hair as she pushed up against him, bringing her breasts against his chest.

Suddenly all he could think of was the feel of them under his hands. He pushed up the silky top she wore until her pale pink bra peeked out at him. He leaned up as he finished exposing the thin lace garment. The fabric was almost transparent. He could barely see the dark ring of her hardened nipples and he knew having them in his hands would not be enough.

Nancy's breathing sped as she watched him hook his finger under the lacy edge and pull, freeing her breast from its confines, then repeated the action on her other breast.

She held perfectly still as he looked at her, bared to him.

"Beautiful." He leaned down and pulled one deep pink tip into his mouth.

Nancy gasped as her fingers dug into his scalp.

Gently he ran his teeth across the nipple before softly stroking the tender flesh with his tongue. She moaned softly.

"That feels so good." Her voice was husky and breathless as she writhed under him.

Oh, he was going to make her feel good. He released her and kissed his way up her neck to stop at her ear.

"Can I touch you?" He slid his hand down her belly so she would understand what he was asking permission for.

"Yes. Please."

He quickly unhooked her pants with a thumb and a finger and slipped his hand inside. It might have been years since she'd been touched in the way he planned on touching her. He should be gentle with her. He should take his time. But he couldn't.

He needed to feel her, make her come. Show her he could give her things no one else could.

He used his knee, parting her legs. He slid his fingers into her panties and immediately sank them deep inside her. She was slick and hot and tight making him groan as he imagined how good she would feel on his dick. If it wasn't such a lazy bastard. He shoved the thoughts of his shortcomings to the side and focused on something he could control. Her coming.

He pulled his fingers back out and spread wetness up and down her slit, rubbing over her clit with each pass he made, dragging a soft moan from deep in her throat. She arched her back, pushing her breasts to him, making it impossible to resist filling his mouth once again.

He licked and nipped at her tightly puckered nipples as he slowly slid his fingers in and out, letting the pad of his thumb rub circles in time with the thrusts. So quickly he felt a tug of disappointment, her thighs began to shake where they pressed against his. Seconds later, her fingers pulled tight in his hair and her body tensed.

He slid inside her body as deep as he could, wanting to feel every bit of her as she clenched around him, coming hot and hard against his hand until she went slack beneath him, her arms heavy as they dragged down to rest across his back.

"I--" Her eyes were closed as she struggled to catch her breath. "That--"

Hopefully her lack of complete sentences was a sign she liked what he did to her because his options were more limited than he cared to admit. Unfortunately his bag of tricks was missing one pretty significant tool.

****

Nancy refolded her napkin and set it on the table. Showing up half an hour early was backfiring in a major way. The time was supposed to give her a chance to collect her thoughts, but instead her anxiety about this meeting with her sister now had ample time to grow into a monster that was chewing her guts into tiny bits.

It didn't surprise her when Carol called first, beating her to the punch. Her phone number was on the sign to the farmer's market making it an easy thing to come by for vendors wanting to rent space. Unfortunately, it didn't bode well for her hopes that Carol was a different person than the self-centered, confrontational, dismissive woman she was before.

Nancy was hoping for a little more time to really process the fact that her sister was back but Carol didn't appear to want to give it to her, pushing Nancy to make time to see her.

And she did because ready or not, Nancy wanted to hear what Carol had to say. What explanation she had for sleeping with Sam. What possible reason she could concoct for abandoning Rich. That's why she was here. To give Carol a chance to explain and maybe even apologize.

Not that it would be believed, but at least it would be something. Maybe it would even help Nancy keep moving forward.

Unless of course it pushed her violently backward into the past she was working so hard to get over.

The bell on the diner door chimed. Nancy looked up as Carol walked in, looking around. When she saw Nancy she smiled, uncertainty heavy in her eyes, keeping her lips tight as she walked toward the table.

"Hi." Carol slid her expensive looking buttery leather purse across the booth seat before sliding in beside it. "How are you?"

"Fine." Nancy forced a smile and resisted the urge to automatically reciprocate. How Carol was didn't matter to her. Not right now anyway.

"How is your foot?"

"It is also fine." Nancy studied her sister. She hadn't really taken the time to look at her the other day. She looked hard. The lack of movement in her forehead and around her eyes did nothing to help matters.

Carol shifted in her seat. "That's good. How did you hurt it?"

"I tripped." This small talk was getting old. Nancy didn't want to chat about the weather. She was here for one reason and one reason only.

To decide if she should even consider letting Carol back in her life. In all of their lives.

"Why are you here Carol?" Nancy leaned back in her seat, waiting. Dealing with her sister was always a delicate balance and there was no reason to expect it to be any different now.

As a teenager all it took was one wrong word and Carol would blow up, stomp her feet and say vicious hurtful things until Nancy backed off, letting her younger sister win. It just wasn't worth the fight.

But times had changed.

She had changed.

Now there were things worth fighting for.

Carol took a deep breath, her eyes never leaving Nancy. "I told you. I came back to help you."

Nancy raised one eyebrow. "No." She leaned forward, resting her arms on the table between them. "I want to know why you're really here."

Carol swallowed and her eyes widened almost imperceptibly. She licked her lips as the seconds ticked by, her eyes never wavering.

But Nancy's didn't either. Not until their stare down was interrupted by a waitress taking drink orders.

Finally, when the waitress left to get their colas, Carol cleared her throat. "My life has become complicated and it made me start looking back at the things I've done." She took her glass from the waitress before the woman could even set it on the table and swallowed a few gulps before continuing. "It was a difficult thing to realize it was my own fault I was miserable."

Nancy looked at her expensively groomed sister. Between a perfect haircut, pricey clothes and immaculate manicure, it was tough to imagine her life could be that difficult. By all appearances, Carol had everything she'd wanted.

Money.

"Exactly how has your life become complicated?" Nancy couldn't keep the skepticism from her voice. Not that she tried.

Carol shrugged. "I have been with the same man for a while now and I'm just not sure it's working for me anymore."

"That's why you're back here?" Nancy opened her straw and dropped it into her glass. She wasn't sure what she was expecting when she came here, but so far Carol was leaving her underwhelmed. No apology. No real explanation. And most importantly, only a vague sense of ownership over her actions. Even then, only in how they affected her own life.

It was looking like the same old Carol was sitting in the booth across from her.

"That's part of it. I really did want to come back for a long time, but I figured it would do more harm than good. When I heard about..." She swallowed. "When I heard you'd lost Thomas, I thought maybe now was my chance. I could help you. Try to make up for all the pain I caused when I left."

Nancy shook her head. "That's not really an option for you anymore." The person she hurt the most was gone.

Carol's eyes dropped to her lap.

"Do you know how Rich died?" Nancy wasn't going to give her sister a break because she was sad. Nancy was sad all the time and Carol needed to know just how deep the results of her actions ran. How huge the fallout of her decisions was for people besides herself.

"I heard he was trying to hurt Thomas." Carol's voice was low as she looked at her hands.

"He tried to kill Thomas. More than once."

Carol nodded. "Because he wanted the money from the farm." She looked up. "Money he wouldn't have gotten anyway."

"I thought you might come home when dad died." Nancy needed to change the subject before she became emotional. Rich was still a difficult topic, especially with the person she blamed most for his death sitting in front of her.

Carol took a deep breath. "I know. I just didn't think it would do anyone any good."

"Where have you been all this time?"

The waitress arrived with the two slices of pie they ordered before her sister could answer the question.

Carol rubbed her hands together before grabbing her fork. "Oh my gosh this looks good." She took a bite and rolled her eyes dramatically. "It is good." She chewed for a second then gave a little snort. "Do you remember when we tried to make rhubarb pie and it ended up being soup?"

Nancy was beginning to wonder if she would ever get the answers she was looking for out of Carol. She chewed her own pie slowly, listening to her sister babble about some pie making fiasco they had as children and wondering if her sister was actually sorry for the things she'd done.

And where that answer would leave her.

SEVENTEEN

BETH'S GLASS HUNG in the air, frozen halfway to her parted lips. Her clear blue eyes were wide with the shock resulting from the blow Nancy just hurled at her.

Nancy was up all night thinking long and hard about how to tell Beth that Carol was not only alive and breathing, but back in town to upheave both their lives.

At least it kept her mind off the fact that she hadn't heard from Paul in a few days, but if it meant an easier life for Beth and the girls, she would have happily laid in bed crying on her pillow over the man.

Maybe not happily.

Nancy looked around the high-top bar table, waiting for one of the other women to say something. That was why, after much deliberation, she decided the best way to tell Beth about Carol was with Autumn and Mina, and it wasn't only for Beth. She would need the support of her friends as much as Beth would.

Beth set her glass back on the table as the look of shock on her face twisted into one of confusion. She looked from face to face. First Mina, then Autumn, until finally Beth's gaze landed on Nancy. Her expression changed once again. This time to concern.

"Are you okay?"

Mina and Autumn turned to look at Nancy, then back at Beth. Finally Autumn leaned in to Beth and looked back toward Nancy. "I don't think she heard you."

Beth cocked one eyebrow. "She heard me. She just doesn't want to admit she's not okay."

Nancy slouched in her chair. "It's not that I'm not okay. I just can't believe it and I've been so worried *you* wouldn't be okay." Nancy twisted the paper wrapper from her straw into knots. "I just don't know how to feel about her being here."

"Pissed." Mina's brows were low as she crossed her arms across her chest.

Beth shook her head. "Relieved."

Mina looked at Beth as if she'd lost her mind. "Relieved? How's that?"

Beth shrugged. "Now she can have some answers." Beth finally took a sip from her forgotten soda then rested her arms on the table and leaned against them. "You have a history with Carol. I don't."

Beth's eyes were intense as they stayed glued to Nancy. "I think this is a chance for you to get the answers you want from her and really, finally put the past to bed."

Was that even possible? And if it was, did she even really want to know? So far the answer to that was no. If she did want to know why Sam and Carol had an affair, Nancy would have looked for the answer in the box of letters her sister carelessly left behind all those years ago, but instead they sat untouched on her bedroom floor. She never made it past the first few.

Even that was enough to give her a pretty good idea why Sam and Carol were together.

Ego. But it wasn't his.

"I just don't know if it even matters anymore." The words sounded half-hearted even to her own ears and her friends picked up on it immediately.

Mina shook her head and Beth rolled her eyes as Autumn shot her a skeptical look.

Nancy huffed a sigh. "I don't know that she would even tell the truth." Carol was always one who could give a sympathetic spin to anything. Twist things around until the favorable light shined down on her.

All through high-school, when Nancy's days of being a stand-in for their mother were no longer appreciated, Carol always had a way of coming out of a manure farm smelling like a daisy. Even the night she spent in jail after a fight with a local boy, which Carol won by the way, disappeared. A case of he-said, she-said.

Carol said she was protecting another girl from unwanted advances. Of course the boy she was 'protecting' her from was Carol's boyfriend at the time. After that, the rumor mill around town started buzzing and Carol's life got a whole lot more interesting.

"That's true." Beth flagged the waitress. "But it would be interesting to see why she's here."

Nancy waited for the waitress to leave with their order before filling Beth in on what little she knew about Carol's unexpected appearance. "Carol said she came back because Thomas died. She wanted to help me."

Beth nodded slowly. "Wrong son."

"Yeah." Nancy swallowed. "I don't know why she would want to help me now. I needed help when the boys were young. Where was she then?" The anger Nancy worked hard to keep in check since the day Carol showed up on her porch, threatened to rear its ugly head.

243

REGRET

The last thing she wanted to do was waste any more energy on her sister than she had to. Carol didn't deserve it.

"Maybe she's changed." Beth shrugged. "Then again, maybe she hasn't. Only one way to find out."

Nancy was almost scared to ask. "How's that?"

Beth waited as the food arrived, then took a big bite of her salad before explaining. "I think we should have dinner one night. Me and the girls, Mina and Thomas and the kids and you and Carol. That way we can all feel her out, maybe put some pressure on her."

"I don't think that's a good idea to have the kids involved until we know just how long she'll stick around." Nancy couldn't bear the thought of Carol hurting more little hearts.

Beth snorted. "Why? She's nothing to the kids besides your sister." Beth stopped with a forkful of salad halfway to her mouth. Her eyes narrowed. "You know *you're* their grandma, don't you?"

A sudden flood of emotion threatened to ruin Nancy's appetite and potentially the whole night. Nancy blinked hard as she swallowed mouthfuls of freezing cold cola, trying to calm the tightness in her throat.

Beth dropped her fork into the salad bowl in front of her. "Shit. This all makes more sense now." She pointed at Nancy. "Carol is nothing," Beth swung her finger around the table, "to any of us, or our children. You are their grandmother and our mother-in-law, not her." Beth paused and looked at Autumn. "Except for her. You're just her friend."

"I wish you were my mother-in-law." Autumn grimaced. "Mine is a—"

Nancy held up a hand. "You don't need to tell me." Jerry's mom was a well-known bad-mouther, frequently at Autumn's expense and regularly at everyone else's. "She wanders all around the farmer's market bad-mouthing anyone who won't come down on their prices just for her."

"Well at least it's not just me." Autumn took a bite of chicken finger and covered her full mouth with one hand. "Still, she's a pain in my ass."

Beth waved her hands dismissively. "We've established you're great, everyone loves you, and Carol and Autumn's mother-in-law suck." Autumn propped her chin on her hands, elbows on the table. "What I really want to know now is, how's Paul?"

Nancy looked at her plate, hoping she could poke an answer out of her baked potato with her fork as she stabbed at the fluffy, buttery flesh. No luck.

"Fine I guess."

Mina groaned. "I'll kill him."

Nancy tipped her head Mina's way and gave her a skeptical look. "You can't kill him." She bit the head off a floret of perfectly cooked broccoli. "Not until after Thomas' house is finished."

"I don't know…" Autumn looked thoughtful. "If she kills him before, we could just dump him in when they pour the foundation." The red-head nodded. "Yeah. That's how they got rid of Jimmy Hoffa."

Nancy looked around the table of women and couldn't help but smile. They were her friends. Come hell or high water, these women had her back. Right now they were discussing how to murder and dispose of a man who wronged her. That was real friendship.

"It is what it is." Nancy set her napkin on the table beside her plate. "I guess I was just more interested in him than he was in me."

All three women shook their heads.

"Why in the world would he just drop off the face of the Earth then?" Nancy pulled out her wallet as the waitress reappeared. "That makes no sense."

"Men make no sense." Mina fished through her giant purse.

"Ain't that the truth?" Their waitress snorted. "Not eavesdropping." She passed out bills. "Just commiserating."

The young woman left to process their payments and Nancy popped her complimentary mint in her mouth. "So what do I do?"

"Nothing." Beth smiled.

"Nothing?" Maybe being single all these years was a blessing in disguise.

Autumn grinned along with Beth. "You wait."

Nancy threw her hands up. Now they weren't making any sense either. "For what?"

Autumn giggled. "For him to figure it out."

****

"You're awfully quiet this morning."

"Just trying to get done." Paul tucked his pencil behind his ear and pushed up off his knees to head out the front door. Now that the weather finally caught up with the calendar, he could prop open the front door, letting the lingering scent of paint and plaster blow away with the breeze. If only it would take his shitty disposition with it.

You would think, after all these years of dreaming about it, having Nancy Richards in his hands would have put him in a much better mood. Maybe if it happened before when he could do something about it, it might have. But as of now, it was only pissing him off.

He stomped off the low porch and lined the three-foot piece of baseboard up along the bridge of his saw, then pulled the blade down through the wood and walked back to the house.

The job he was stuck doing today wasn't helping his mood either. Laying trim was his least favorite activity. At least it meant they were on the home stretch. And not a second too soon. The guys were scheduled to start digging the new foundation of Thomas' house next week and Paul wanted to be there to make sure things went the way he wanted.

Paul brushed past Mina and crouched down to line up the baseboard he'd just cut. He reached for the nail gun, but his hand only found the thick brown paper protecting the high-grade laminate they'd installed last week.

"Why are you acting like an ass?"

Mina stood a few feet away, the nailer in her hand, one eyebrow up.

"I'm not an ass."

"I didn't say you were an ass. I said you were acting like an ass."

He held out his hand.

She took a breath, her nostrils flaring, before she relented and handed him the tool.

This was one of the many reasons he'd used as an excuse to keep his distance from Nancy. Mixing business and personal relations was a bad idea. In this case especially bad because the very things that made him love Mina were making her a serious pain in his ass right now.

He held the baseboard in place as he pushed the tip of the gun against the wood. "I'm not sure what you're talking about."

She made some sort of a snorting noise. He ignored her and focused all his attention on attaching the baseboard to the wall, running a long, loud line of air-propelled nails through the trim.

He held back a smile as the noises kept coming. This one was a scoff, maybe. At least he was aggravating her almost as much as she was aggravating him.

"What do you mean you have no idea what I'm talking about?"

He stood up. "I'm not sure what you're talking about unless it's something that's none of your business."

"None of my business?" Mina crossed her arms and stood her ground. Paul stood a head taller and a good hundred pounds more, but he knew without a doubt, if she ever wanted to, this woman could most certainly put a hurting on him. It had been one of his favorite things about her. When the woman's feathers were ruffled, she'd take on anything. Now that he was on the receiving end, it was less endearing.

"Your trying to nose around in things you don't understand." He tried to walk past her to retrieve another length of baseboard, but she sidestepped and blocked his path.

"You're right about that. I can't understand why you are being like this." She paused. "Especially to her."

Damn. He'd been doing pretty well with avoiding this conversation with Mina, but from the looks of it, she had no intention of relenting this time and she knew exactly which buttons to push.

"I haven't done anything to her." That was a big part of the problem. He stared Mina down, clinging to the last little bit of hope he had that he could get her to drop this.

She scowled up at him, one hundred percent unintimidated by his attempt to back her off. "You can't just disappear on her and act like that's not going to be a problem."

"I've been busy."

Mina rolled her eyes. "Doing what? Your schedule is so full you can't even give her a quick call?"

She pointed her finger and stabbed it in his direction. "You used to be fun and laid back and happy. Now you're just... just..."

He crossed his arms and waited to hear just what she thought he'd become because he didn't even know anymore. Life used to be quiet and boring and lonely, but at least it was easy. All the time he spent imagining a life with Nancy and never once did he consider how fucking hard it would turn out to be.

Mina raised her hands as she finally found the word she'd been searching for.

"Miserable."

"That doesn't make any sense." He tried again to get around her. Once again, she sidestepped and blocked his path.

"I agree. So why is it the truth?"

"It's not." Why was she pushing this? He knew what he was and what he wasn't.

She nodded her head. "Oh it definitely is, but for the life of me I can't figure out why. You've loved her for forever and things are finally working out for you guys. You should be thrilled." She paused and narrowed her amber eyes at him. "But you're not, and you need to figure out why before you ruin this."

She took a step toward him. "She's been through so much Paul. She deserves a man who loves her like he's never loved anything."

Her words trapped the air in his lungs.

REGRET

He couldn't do what she was asking. What he knew Nancy deserved.

He couldn't love her completely. With his heart, yes. That was something he'd done for years. But there was more to a relationship than that. You could say there wasn't. That love was enough, but it wasn't.

Mina was right. Nancy deserved to be loved completely. And as much as he wanted to believe he could be the man to give that to her, the truth was, he probably wasn't.

Not because he didn't want to, because he did. With every fiber of his being, he wanted to love Nancy in ways she never knew were possible. He wanted to make her his in every way. He wanted to show her how a real man treats the woman he calls his.

His body however, had other ideas.

"I'm not talking about this with you." He pushed past Mina and out the door. He needed to get out of here before he lost his mind.

His shortcomings were all he thought about as it was. The last thing he needed were people pointing them out.

Paul slammed the door on his truck as the engine roared to life. He backed down the driveway faster than he should making his tires squeal as he swung onto the road and threw it into drive.

He was acting like a hot-headed kid and he knew it. If only he had the dick to match. He slammed his fist onto the dashboard in frustration. He wasted the best years of his life on women that didn't matter like they should have. Like they deserved to.

Maybe this was his penance for being with them when he knew they could never be what he wanted. Maybe he deserved this.

He looked up as the small block building where he spent many lonely evenings drinking away his life came into view.

He shouldn't be here, but right now, this place held the only thing that had any potential to make him forget that what he'd waited so many years to get his hands on was likely going to slip right through his fingers.

EIGHTEEN

"THIS IS REALLY good Nancy." Carol shoved another bite of cake into her mouth.

Nancy didn't tell her if she kept eating it like she was, her sister's svelte figure would soon be a distant memory. Instead she just smiled.

The evening was going remarkably well all things considered. The house was full of most of the people she loved most.

And Carol.

Thomas and Mina brought the kids and Beth was there with the girls. All to 'meet Carol'. Any suspicious looks from Beth or Mina appeared to go unnoticed, at least by Carol. Nancy caught and appreciated each one.

Beth hit the nail on the head at dinner. One of the main fears she had about Carol showing up was that she would sweep in and steal Liza and Kate right out from under her. For some reason, she worried biology would trump all. That because of Carol's mere presence, they could no longer be hers. It was a stupid fear that seemed even dumber now that she saw Carol around the kids.

It was like they had the plague. And head lice. And maybe a booger on their finger.

If any one of them came near her, she would scoot away quickly, keeping a close eye on the offending child until there were at least ten feet between them.

Nancy considered telling Carol the cake she was enjoying so much had toddler spit in it, but decided that was a fun secret to keep to herself. It made each bite her sister savored a pleasure to watch.

"Maybe you can teach me to cook." Carol licked the last of the frosting off her fork. "I'm still terrible at it."

Nancy collected the girls' abandoned plates from the table and deposited them in the sink. "It just takes practice."

Carol stacked the remaining dishes on the table. "Well, maybe when I get a more permanent place with a kitchen I can start working on that."

Nancy's eyes widened and the food she'd managed to get down tightened into a solid ball in her stomach. "You're staying?"

Carol picked up the stack of plates. "Well... yes." She walked slowly to the sink. "I just thought, maybe it would be good to be," she set the dishes on the counter, "with my family."

She chewed her lip as she looked at Nancy. "I was hoping you would give me the chance to make up for all the awful things I've done, but if you can't, I understand."

Nancy wanted to say no. It was too late. She'd hurt too many people in too many ways and she needed to go back to wherever she came from. Maybe give her a nice shove as she walked away.

But if Carol left now, she would take the only chance Nancy might have at closure on more than a couple important issues. Like why she fucked her husband for starters. Followed closely by why she left, abandoning not just her son, but her whole family. Nancy would put money down the two were related.

Nancy switched on the faucet and started to fill the sink. The farmhouse was old enough there wasn't a good spot to stick a dishwasher. She usually didn't mind, but when she had company, it would really come in handy to just push a button.

"I don't know what's going to happen Carol." She pulled a fresh dishrag from the cabinet and tossed it into the steaming, sudsy water. "There's a lot of hurt there and I just don't know if I can get past it."

Nancy certainly didn't have a great history when it came to getting past things. She was trying, but it was a hard thing to do. Forgiving other people's mistakes would make it ridiculous to not forgive her own and that was a major hang-up and apparently not just for her.

A lump formed in her throat. She focused on wiping the cloth around the plate in her hand. Scrubbing away the bits of food clinging to the white porcelain. Her hands turned pink in the almost scalding water. She hoped the discomfort could steal her thoughts away from the man who managed to bring her equal amounts of happiness, pleasure, and unfortunately now pain.

"I think it's clean." Carol's voice snapped her attention from the man she was trying so hard to avoid thinking about, yet still managed to be the only thing to easily occupy her mind.

"Sorry. I zoned out for a minute there." She rinsed the dish under cool water in the other bowl of the porcelain double sink. Carol took it gently and began drying it off with a towel she'd grabbed from the counter.

"I noticed." She placed the plate on the counter and held her hand out for the one Nancy was rinsing. "Want to talk about it?"

Nancy almost laughed. She did want to talk about it, but certainly not with a woman she didn't trust any further than she could throw her. Unfortunately, there was really no point in talking about it with anyone.

The only person she should actually talk to about it wasn't much of a talker. Really, at all. Any time the conversation got even a little deep he ran like he was on fire. As much as it was breaking her heart, that was not the kind of man she wanted.

Did he have valid reasons for his behavior? Probably, but she'd never know because he wouldn't freaking talk to her about it.

She handed Carol the plate and went in for another. "No thanks."

Thankfully, Carol easily moved into a mostly one-sided conversation about the things around town that had changed while she was gone. Occasionally Nancy offered a couple words to avoid being a complete bitch. Carol was just trying to fill the time while they finished washing the dishes. She should be grateful for the help and the conversation but Carol's small talk was aggravating when they had so many big things to discuss.

She hurried through the pots and pans. Carol's constant chattering was wearing on her. At least she was self-aware enough to realize it was her, not her sister who was the current problem.

Who the fuck did Paul think he was?

Did he think he could just slip in and out of her life whenever he wanted? How could he seem so interested in her one minute and the next, she didn't hear from him for days.

The last time she saw him he'd given her the first orgasm she'd had that wasn't at her own hands. She thought he was finally past whatever was going on in his head. Why else would he be so passionate with her? What was the purpose of doing that to her and then just disappearing?

He wouldn't even let her return the damn favor. What kind of man insists on pleasing you, denying himself, and then stops calling?

Nancy pulled the plug on the drain and wrung out the dishcloth. It felt good to strangle something, even if it was just an innocent hunk of cotton.

Paul's behavior shouldn't have surprised her. In the short amount of time they'd been what she would consider, exploring their relationship, he'd been more than a little skittish and it was making her consider a possibility that was more depressing than she wanted to admit.

Maybe the Paul that lived in her mind, and the real Paul were two very different men.

REGRET

The damn lump was back, but this time she was alone. Carol put away the last of the dishes and left to awkwardly join the rest of the family in the front room.

Nancy could hear the kids giggling as Charlie and Maddie played with the younger girls. Normally it would put a smile on her face, but today she couldn't muster up much more than not frowning.

"Please don't tell me you're going to start being a pain in the ass too."

Nancy jumped, bracing her hand over her heart like a startled old lady.

Mina propped against the counter unfazed by the reaction. "I can only handle one at a time and just because Don's building inspection shenanigans are no longer screwing with my life that doesn't free up a spot for you."

"Jesus, you scared me." Nancy turned her back to the sink and leaned against it as she waited for the beating of her heart to slow.

"I was talking to you and thought you were ignoring me. Were you deep in thought?"

Nancy rubbed her temples. She was getting a headache. "I don't even know."

"How's it going?" Mina wrapped her arms over her chest and leaned harder against the island counter, crossing one leg over the other.

"I don't know that either." Nancy rolled her head from side to side. "What about you? How do you think it's going?"

Mina raised her eyebrows and whispered across the island. "The woman does not like kids I can tell you that much." She took a quick glance toward the front room. "Other than that, I'm not getting much from her. She seems really closed off. I don't think she's said much of anything to anyone besides you."

"I just don't know why in the heck she's back here." She and Carol were close as children, but once puberty hit and Carol could fend for herself, she did, leaving Nancy in her wake, cleaning up her messes and dealing with her discarded responsibilities. It didn't make sense that their relationship would be a reason to return. "And she seems so calm."

"I don't know. I do know age changes people." Mina got quiet for a second then looked up at Nancy. "Do you think she's sick?"

That never occurred to Nancy. It would be one of the few explanations that made sense. Maybe Carol was here to make peace with the life and the people she left behind.

And screwed over.

****

REGRET

Paul felt sick as the excess of liquid in his stomach sloshed around. Drinking was harder than he remembered it being. Maybe if it was doing a more accurate job of making him forget the shit in his life, he wouldn't mind how big of a pain in the ass it was. But it wasn't, so he was stuck listening to the sound of his own slurred words and thinking about Nancy.

Her and his broken fucking dick.

The bar around him erupted as the game on the television got interesting. Interesting to them anyway. He couldn't give two shits about some fucking punk kid who could make a cool mil for throwing a ball. His dick probably worked too. He was probably fucking a different girl every night. Prick probably didn't appreciate it either.

It wasn't fair. All those year he wasted on other women. Wasn't fair to him, wasn't fair to them, wasn't fair to his Nancy.

Fuck. She wasn't his. Never was, now never could be. He couldn't make her his. Not in the way she deserved and from the way things seemed the other night, the way she wanted.

It had been a long time since Paul had been intimate in any sort of a way with a woman. The last time was the night his issues came fully into the light.

Paul downed half the remaining whiskey in his glass, savoring the burn as it slid down, trying to dull the sting of the memory.

It would have been the last time he tried to be with a woman, even if the one in question had been a little more understanding about the situation. As it was, she didn't take to kindly to a man being unable to get a hard on at the sight of her naked body stretched before him.

He understood her reaction. Tried to explain it wasn't her, it was him, but she didn't want to hear it. She threw his pants in his face and ordered him out of her life.

He went home that night and vowed never to be in that position again, but he'd been stupid enough to come dangerously close in recent weeks. Maybe it was because he knew Nancy would never throw him out. Never become irate with his lack of function. Her sweetness weakened his resolve to the point he almost convinced himself it could work. They could work. He could make her happy in other ways.

Then he saw just how sexually functional she was. He hadn't been ready for the way she reacted to his touch. The way she moved. The way she moaned. How very, very ready her body was for anything he would want to do to her.

He also wasn't ready for the anger that bubbled up inside him. The frustration he felt when he discovered just how much he would have to deny her. Exactly how much she needed and wanted the one thing he couldn't give her.

He finished the last of his drink and knocked on the bar. Within seconds, the bartender was standing across from him, eyeing him heavily.

"You sure you need another?"

All it took was two seconds of remembering Nancy's words, whispered in his ear, full of longing and needed. Words that changed everything.

"Yup."

The bartender stood still for a second longer, studying him for signs of over serving. It was not something he was used to. A few months ago, his desire for another drink was never even questioned, so why now? Especially since he needed that drink now more than ever.

Finally a tumbler slid across the smooth wood bar. To prove his point, Paul downed it in one take, licking his lips as he set the empty glass heavily on the bar. He closed his eyes and waited for the liquor to sink in. He really needed it too. And soon. Erase those soft sweet words that played over and over in his mind.

'I want you.'

Paul felt the bar around him gently begin turning on some unseen axis. The sounds filling the room, the voices, the gentle clinking of glasses and bottles, faded as he began to float.

"You all right Paul?" The bartender's voice jolted him from his first moments of peace in months.

He opened his eyes and scowled. "Fine."

The man raised his eyebrow. "You don't look fine."

"I am." Paul lowered his brows. He wasn't here to socialize.

The bartender shook his head. "I gotta cut you off."

"Whatever." He pushed away from the bar.

"You can't drive Paul. Don't make me call the cops."

"I'm not fucking driving." His words sounded messy and barely coherent even to him. "I gotta piss."

It took all his remaining brain power to put one foot in front of the other, but he moved through the bar without a stumble. Barely.

It wasn't until the cool night air hit his face that he realized he was not in the men's room.

He rolled his head back to the sky and squeezed his hands into tight fists at his sides. "Fuuuuuuuuuck!"

He took a breath and tried to regain some of the clarity he was attempting to drown in fermented liquid less than five minutes ago. Unfortunately, his equally over-served bladder couldn't wait any longer. He blinked hard, trying to get a clear look at his surroundings.

Cars were still moving up and down the road outside the bar and a few pedestrians were scattered on the sidewalk. Sitting in the darkened bar, he'd thought it was late, but maybe he was wrong.

He looked around, his limited vision zoning in on a narrow alleyway that ran beside the block building that housed the bar and connected the downtown to a more residential area. That is where he would leave the contents of his bladder.

Paul started to walk and realized that last drink, the one he took in one gulp to prove a point, was just beginning to slap him around. He had to use one hand to brace his tipping body against the building as he walked.

Barely reaching the corner, Paul was thumbing the button of his jeans when he slammed into a guy coming down the narrow passage. The force of their bodies crashing together almost knocked him back on his ass. Luckily, one hand was still on the wall and he managed to keep himself upright.

"Sorry." Paul squinted as he tried to get a better look at the man standing in front of him. He looked almost like—

"Sam?"

The man's eyes were wide as he looked from one side of Paul to the other.

The motherfucker who ruined his life, stole his only chance at happiness, was looking for a way to run. Like a scared little girl. The combination of the narrow alley and the width of Paul's shoulders left him no options besides turning to run, which had apparently not yet occurred to him.

"You son of a bitch." Paul swung as hard as he could, his body spinning with the momentum. He didn't even get the chance to enjoy the thud as his fist connected with the man's face before the whole world went black.

NINETEEN

PAUL'S TONGUE WAS swollen and dry in his mouth. Almost as swollen and dry as the eyelids he had to peel open, making them scrape roughly against his corneas, to squint against the glaring sunlight.

He looked around the cab of his truck. The grey block wall of the establishment where he spent his evening stared at him through the windshield. He remembered parking his truck in this spot and walking through the heavy metal door, but the rest of his night was pretty blurry, including how he ended up right back where he started.

Running his hands over his eyes he tried to rub away the confusion and grit left from a night of heavy drinking.

He grunted as the movement revealed a deep ache in his right hand. Holding it up in front of his face he slowly opened and closed his fingers making a half-hearted fist. A faint bruise marred the top of his knuckles and the back of his palm. For a second, a hazy memory teased him from the edge of his mind.

Just when it felt close enough to grasp, a torn square of college ruled paper tucked in between the buttons of his shirt stole his attention. Messy scrawls that ran perpendicular to the thin blue lines explained that his old drinking buddies found him passed out on the sidewalk and shoved him in his truck to sleep it off.

They were also nice enough to leave a bottle of water on his dash.

Throwing the note to the floorboards, he started to twist open the cap, forgetting his bruised hand until a stab of pain reminded him. He switched hands and chugged half the bottle, the water both soothing and burning his raw throat.

He shouldn't have gone to the bar last night. Or the night before for that matter, but at least then he held his liquor.

Last night he was out of control. It was shameful. It was irresponsible. And it fixed nothing.

He leaned his throbbing head back against the headrest. If anything, his little relapse only made things worse. He tipped the bottle to his lips and drank the rest, hoping the extra hydration would ease his roaring headache.

The sun assaulting his eyes was also heating up the cab as it crept higher in the sky and the increasing warmth made him feel dangerously close to puking. He crammed his hand into his pocket praying his keys were still there. When his fingers raked across the grooved metal, he wanted to smile, but resisted. Any movement of his face would likely make his head explode.

He shoved the key into the ignition and cranked them a half twist, his other hand pushing the window button at the same time. Cool outside air blew gently over his face. He took a deep breath, hoping to push down the urge to vomit as he tried to determine if he was still drunk.

He must have dozed back off because the sound of a truck backing up beside him startled him awake, his head pulsing with each beep of the accompanying warning. At least this time, he felt a little better as he woke up, less sick and more coherent.

The clock on his dash read 1:00.

"Shit."

He turned the ignition the rest of the way over and searched the glove compartment for a pair of sunglasses. Normally he went without, but today they were necessary. More than.

Shoving a pair of old, bent shades on his face, Paul backed out of the lot and went home intending to fall directly into bed and try like hell to sleep off the rest of this hangover.

Unfortunately, a nagging memory, floating around in the back of his brain wouldn't let him relax.

He peeled off his clothes and threw the pile of crumpled bar stink into the basket before stepping under a screaming hot stream of water. He scrubbed the stale smell of bar and alcohol off his body as he tried to put the pieces of last night together, hoping it would bring what was worrying him into focus.

He'd had too much that was for sure. He vaguely remembered being cut off. Did he try to leave?

The thought bothered him. In all the nights he'd been overserved, never once did he try to get home behind the wheel. The thought that maybe he'd considered it last night filled him with shame.

Why was he even there? To drink away his problems? He should know by now, that didn't ever fucking work. They were all still here, and sometimes even worse. Like they could have been last night if he succeeded in getting behind the wheel.

Best case scenario, he would have taken himself out. Worst case, someone else.

Paul leaned one arm against the wall as he let the hot water stream over his body.

What was he doing? Still punishing himself for letting Sam have Nancy? For not fighting harder for her? If only he'd had the balls, maybe her life would be different right now. Hell, he would have made sure her life was very different. He would never have slept with her sister for starters. Or threatened to kill her.

His skin felt cold as ice even as the heat from the water turned it a deep pink as memories of last night began to trickle through his mind. He shut the faucet off and stared at the drops of water clinging to the tile as the full memory of last night came rushing back.

Sam.

Paul held up his hand. The bruise had darkened slightly and was creeping up his hand. What had he really seen in the alley? A man? A ghost? A hallucination?

He stepped out of the shower and wrapped his towel around his waist before digging the jeans from last night out of the basket at the door. His phone was still in the back pocket. He walked into his bedroom and woke it up.

No missed calls.

Sitting on the edge of the bed, Paul stared at the screen. What did he expect? He tossed the phone on the blanket beside him and fell back against the mattress, squeezing his head between his hands.

All this anger he had at Sam for hurting Nancy. All his boasting that he would have been better, loved her more, appreciated her.

He was just as bad as Sam. Maybe worse.

He needed to talk to her if she would let him. The chance was pretty slim, but he had to at least try this time instead of just giving up. He tugged on his clothes and almost ran for the door, hoping he hadn't once again lost her. This time for good.

****

The knees of Nancy's jeans clung to her leg as the wetness from the grass transferred to the fabric. She gripped the clump of dandelions in her tulip bed, pulling and twisting at the same time. The greens snapped apart, leaving behind a wad of roots that would bloom again. Probably tomorrow.

"Damn it."

She should go get her hand shovel. Actually she should go change into her work clothes and put on a pair of gloves. Nancy looked down at the smudges on her pants and the almost black dirt caked under her nails. She went back in for another clump. No point changing now. The damage was done.

All she meant to do was drop her mail in the box and go back inside, but there was no way she could ignore the line of weeds staring her in the face as she walked back to the house.

It was time for life to go back to normal. She had a garden to plant, a farm to help run, girls to watch, and flower beds to weed. It was a life most people would be happy to have. A life she should be happy to have. And she was… to a point.

Nancy rocked back on her heels and swiped her forearm at a clump of hair trying to go up her nose. Maybe as time went on she would get back to a point where she was happy with her life, or at least satisfied.

She reached for another, larger clump of weeks next to her favorite rose bush. She wrapped her fingers around and squeezed hard. The thorns from a hidden rose branch the weeds were wrapped around stabbed into her hand.

"Son of a bitch!" She yanked her hand back just as the pinpricks of blood started to color the dirt covering her skin.

"I deserve that."

Paul's voice nearly made Nancy jump out of her skin, bringing her to her feet. She turned around before his presence even registered. Just barely.

Her hand was beginning to throb and she could feel the blood slowly oozing out, but it was quickly being forgotten as an overwhelming mix of anger and sadness bubbled up through her. "Yes, you do."

For so long she imagined Paul as the man who would save her. Save her from the loneliness, the regret, the doubt. He'd done none of those things. If anything he'd reinforced them. Made her pain deeper. The loneliness, lonelier.

She wanted to cry, but refused. She'd cried too many times already. She was done.

"Why are you here?"

Paul's attention focused on her hands. "Are you bleeding?"

"What?" She scoffed. He was going to show up unannounced, the first time she'd heard from him in over a week, and that was what he had to say?

He pointed at her injured hand. "You're bleeding."

She held the hand up. A small trickle made its way down her finger and was forming a drip off the tip. Nancy wiped it on her already dirty jeans. She'd throw them in the wash as soon as Paul left, which meant they'd be in before the blood had a chance to dry. Especially since she was going to ask him some pretty hard questions.

"Why are you here Paul? What do you want from me? You can't keep doing this. I can't—" Her voice caught and she cleared her throat, resigned to her earlier commitment to not crying.

"Nancy I want you." He clenched his hands at his sides. "I always have."

She snorted. "Whatever." She walked toward the porch steps. "I have stuff to do."

"I just don't know that I can give you what you need."

Nancy leaned her head back and took a deep breath. Why in the hell would he drive all the way here to give her the 'it's not you it's me' speech? Probably hoping to keep in good standing with her spitfire of a future daughter-in-law.

She turned to look over her shoulder at him. "And what is it you think I need from you?"

His eyes darted from side to side as he licked his lips, his hands still in fists at his sides. "Can we go inside?"

"For what Paul? You already said it. You can't give me what I need. It's fine. I'm a big girl." Nancy turned away and headed up the steps. Her hand was on the door when his voice stopped her dead in her tracks.

"I can't make love to you."

She turned back to face him, narrowing her eyes. "You're right about that one. That ship has sailed." She felt sick to her stomach. All these years she'd built him up on a pedestal, but it turned out he was just like every other man. Only worried about his dick.

His eyes widened and he shook his head. "No, no. No!" He put his hands up. "I didn't mean it like that." He dropped his hands and his shoulders slumped. "I mean I can't. My..." He closed his eyes. "I just can't."

Did he mean? Nancy thought back to their... interactions. She'd tried to touch him once. The last time she saw him. He'd pushed her hands away and insisted holding her was enough.

She nodded her head toward the house. "Come inside."

Nancy turned to open the door. She kicked off her wet shoes and looked down at the damp jeans clinging to her kneecaps and her injured hand. The bleeding on her hand had stopped, but the pricks would be sore as hell tomorrow if they didn't get cleaned out.

"I'll be right back." She moved quickly up the steps to her bathroom without waiting for a response from Paul.

She shut the door behind her and leaned against it. Slowly her mind began putting together the pieces of the time she and Paul spent together. From the day he whisked her off to pick up Maddie and Charlie at school, to the night she showed up at his house to get the heaters.

What if everything he did, all the contradictions were because of him, not her?

Paul didn't just think he wasn't enough for her sexually. Paul didn't think he was enough for her at all.

She used her elbow to flip the handle on the faucet and began scrubbing her hands as quickly as she could, knowing there was a chance, a substantial one, that when she made it back downstairs, Paul would be gone.

Her heart pounded as she darted into her room and grabbed the first pair of pants she saw, a black pair of joggers she lounged around the house in. She tried to step into them as she walked and almost fell, catching herself on the nightstand before she toppled over.

Nancy blew the hair out of her face and stood still just long enough to get the pants most of the way up. She situated them at her waist as she went quickly back down the stairs, holding her breath a little as the living room came into view.

Paul was still by the front door, his hands in his pockets, staring at the ground, seemingly unaware she was back.

"You could have sat down."

He looked her way and for the first time she noticed the bags under his eyes. The dullness of his skin under a week's worth of stubble. The dryness of his lips.

"What's going on Paul?"

He rubbed his hand over his jaw. The sound of his calloused fingers on his scruff was like sandpaper. "I needed to talk to you."

"Are you impotent?"

Paul started coughing. She waited, resisting the urge to say more. He was the one who came here and he was the one who dropped that bomb a few minutes ago. He would be the one to explain.

His cough turned into a nervous laugh. He took a deep breath and scratched at the back of his neck. Finally, he looked at her, then the ceiling. "Yeah."

She nodded and crossed her arms over her chest. "Do you think that is something I would not be accepting of?"

"It's not fair of me to ask you to be accepting of that."

"Oh." She stood quietly for a minute as things Paul told her flooded her mind. "You've said a lot about what you think is fair to me, what I need, and I'm a little upset that you think you get to decide what I do and don't need. I think maybe it's all an excuse." She dropped her arms and took another step toward him. "Why don't you want to be with me, really?"

"I do want to be with you."

She cocked an eyebrow at him. "Well I hate to tell you this, but if that's the case you've been going about this all wrong."

TWENTY

PAUL LINGERED BY the front door. Stuck in the limbo between the lies he'd built up so carefully and the truth still hanging in the air between them.

Why was everything so damn hard? Hard to admit the truth he'd been avoiding for nearly thirty years. Hard to ignore the lies he'd told himself so long they were more like the truth. Hard to talk to her.

Harder not to.

He spent the drive here thinking about what needed to be said between them but now that she was in front of him it was like his tongue was glued to the top of his mouth.

To be fair, they were discussing his issues with erectile dysfunction which would trip up the best of men, but right now tripped up wasn't something he could afford to be.

This was his Hail Mary. His last shot at the one thing he'd wanted his whole adult life and he was handling the pressure worse than a freshman quarterback.

This was supposed to be where he convinced her to forgive him. To be his, but instead the same old shit was coming out of his mouth. The same old excuses he'd fallen back on for years.

He did want to be with Nancy. More than he'd ever wanted anything. But as much as he wanted it, the idea filled him with an equal amount of terror.

"Relax." Nancy reached out and rested her hands on his arms. Her blue eyes were warm as she looked at him. Not with the pity or disappointment he expected, but something else.

"Just talk to me." She smiled softly. His eyes caught on her lips. Lips that he wanted to kiss every morning and every night. And he could. If he had enough balls to lay it on the line.

Every single bit of it.

"Nan, I love you. I always have." His stomach dropped as he heard the words come out of his mouth. Words that had to be said, but words Paul never thought he would be able to say. Not now. Maybe not ever.

He struggled to breathe as those damned words hung in the air, the weight of all they carried crushing the air from his lungs. His whole life came to a point before his eyes. There would always be two sides. Before and after. The next few seconds would determine which side was the happy one.

"I'm just so confused." Nancy dropped her hands to her sides.

Paul swallowed hard as he tried to not be distracted by how much he missed the feel of her hands on his arms. "I understand. I've made this difficult and you need some time to sort out how you feel about me." He took a step back, giving her some space. "If you feel about me at all."

She laughed and shook her head making her pale blonde hair fall into her face. "That's not what I meant." She stepped forward, taking away the space he gave her. "I just don't know where we go from here." She looked up at him, her blue eyes searching his face before dropping.

She stood quietly for a minute chewing her lip, her face serious. Her eyes finally came back to his. "You know your…" Her eyes dropped to the front of his pants then came back. "You know that doesn't matter to me, right?"

She made it sound so simple. As if it was no big deal, this problem he had.

"It might matter eventually." He avoided her eyes. He hadn't even told his doctor and he sure as hell never wanted to have a conversation like this with Nancy. It was more than uncomfortable, worse than just embarrassing. He was telling the woman he loved, the woman he was asking to love him, that he wasn't really a man. Not a complete one.

And then asking her to love him anyway.

She tipped her head to one side. "No. It won't." She studied him. "Would it matter to you if I couldn't and you could?"

"No." The word came out louder and more forceful than he expected making Nancy jump ever so slightly.

The idea that he would care about what she could and couldn't do for him sexually was so offensive that it was a knee-jerk reaction.

She smiled. "That's how I feel about it. It hurts my feelings a little that you would think something as small as that--" Her eyes flew open. "That came out wrong."

Paul laughed out loud. He grabbed Nancy and wrapped her in his arms as she continued trying to explain what she meant to say.

"I didn't mean it was small. I meant the issue was small."

He hugged her tighter, enjoying the feel of her against him without any fear or panic lingering in the back of his mind, a smile still on his face. "I love you."

This time the words came easy. It was about time something did.

Nancy's head was buried in his shoulder. "It's a good thing."

He pulled back, looking at her face, still a little flushed from embarrassment. "It's a very good thing."

She squinted at him. "In that case, can I ask why you look like shit?"

"I had a little bit of a rough night." His head started to ache at the memory of the hangover four Motrin were barely keeping at bay.

"Last night?"

He rocked his head from side to side. "Maybe the last few nights."

Nancy cocked an eyebrow at him. "You need to learn to cope with things better."

Paul leaned down and brushed his lips across hers for the first time in days. It was longer than he ever wanted to go without kissing her again. "I'm working on it."

She laughed. "Fair enough." She wrapped her arms around his neck, and leaned in to kiss him back. It made him think maybe she missed him as much as he missed her.

Her lips lingered against his as her fingers trailed across the thick stubble covering his jaw. Her touch was so soft, so gentle he could feel the tension easing free of his tightly strung limbs.

By the time she pulled away, he felt like putty. All the fear, the frustration, the anger, gone.

And then she unknowingly brought it all back.

"Tell me about your night." She smiled up at him, clueless.

"You don't happen to have any coffee made do you?"

She raised her eyebrows. "That bad?"

He nodded. "Pretty bad."

She grabbed his hand and pulled him gently in the direction of the kitchen. "Hungry?"

Paul grabbed his stomach as it started to roll at the thought of food. He never thought he would turn down a meal that came from her kitchen, but he was wrong.

"You should eat some toast too or coffee will tear the lining of your stomach up even more." Nancy pushed gently on his shoulders, easing him into a chair at the kitchen table.

He closed his eyes and listened to her soft humming as she quietly moved around the kitchen. The smell of fresh coffee and browning bread filled the room around him.

This was what he thought of when he imagined a life with Nancy. Nothing fancy. Nothing out of the ordinary.

That was what he wanted. An ordinary life, drinking coffee and eating toast with her across the table from him.

"Hey."

He opened his eyes to Nancy's hand on his shoulder. She nodded to the table. "Why don't you try to eat before you fall asleep?"

Paul picked up the heavy mug she'd placed in front of him and sipped at the smooth cup of coffee. "I was just relaxing for a second."

She snorted as she pulled out the chair beside him and sat down. "You were snoring." Her eyes stayed fixed on him as he slowly bit off a chunk of toast. "You did have a rough night.

He swallowed down the slightly buttery wad of chewed bread. It hung in his throat as the memory of Sam's face lingered in his mind. It was crazy to even consider that last night was anything more than the delusions of a whiskey laced mind, giving him a place to direct the rage he'd held onto all these years.

But could whiskey dream up the Sam stamped in his memory? Because the face haunting him now, wasn't that of the young man who died in a fiery car crash leaving behind a wife, a clandestine lover and two boys.

It was of an aged man.

And until he had a better grasp on last night's evens, it wasn't something he wanted to share with Nancy. If she was his, and he hoped more than anything she was, it was his job to protect her, not upset her for what was certainly no reason.

Nancy's brow furrowed. "What happened to your hand?"

****

Paul looked a little like a deer caught in the headlights, his glassy, wide-eyed stare moving from his hand to her face, then back to his black and blue fist. It took too long for him to find an answer so she decided to ask more questions. See if there was one that could get his brain moving.

"What did you punch?" Nancy took his hand in hers and gently stretched out his fingers to examine his purple, swollen knuckles. "And who ended up worse off?"

Paul picked up his coffee and took a drink. The man was stalling. The question was why. After so much blatant honesty involving some pretty touchy topics, it was a little surprising he would hold back now.

It was no secret in town that Paul had been in his fair share of bar brawls over the years but from what she'd heard his actions were always justified. Usually, it was over a man disrespecting a woman.

"Paul, we don't live in a town that is good at keeping secrets. I know this isn't the first time this has happened." Her intent was to put him at ease, but her words only seemed to confuse him.

His forehead wrinkled, bringing his brows together. "The first time what has happened?"

"The fight." She pointed to his obviously injured hand. "I know there have been other fights over the years."

His slightly ashen color pinked up. Paul's head dropped to his hand as his fingers massaged his temple. "Nan, I couldn't handle the way men would talk about you and it did lead to some..." He cleared his throat. "Altercations."

The way men talked about her? "What do you mean, about me?"

Paul's head snapped up. "Oh. I thought that was--"

"That was why you fought. Me?" She'd felt so alone for years. Thinking no one was there for her.

She was wrong.

Someone was.

Nancy swallowed around the tightness in her throat. There had been too many tears in her life lately, she was done crying them, even if they were happy ones.

She stared down at their hands, stacked together. His hand felt warm and strong under hers. It was a hand that defended her honor even when it didn't matter. Even when no one knew but him. "Paul, I..." She didn't have the right words so she settled for, "You're a good man."

He looked at her as he took another bite of the toast she made him. "I think you would get some argument on that." Paul washed down the mouthful he was still chewing with the last of the coffee in his cup and leaned away from the table.

"From the guy you punched last night?" Nancy imagined the look on the guys face when he realized Paul was coming for him. The man probably crapped his pants. "I would have been interested to see how that played out."

Paul shifted in his seat, his eyes darting around the room, landing everywhere except on her face. Nancy raised an eyebrow. Something was up.

"Who did you hit?"

Paul scratched at the side of his head. "I'm not entirely sure."

"Not entirely?"

He finally looked at her. "No."

Nancy chuckled. "Maybe you gave the wall a hell of a wake-up call."

Paul shrugged his shoulders. "That's what it gets for talking about your ass."

TWENTY-ONE

AUTUMN WAS GIVING Nancy a run for her money. The woman had some serious get up and go to her. Probably a necessity to keep up with the four boys running laps through the fenced yard with Kate and Liza trailing behind them.

"They are going to sleep good tonight." Nancy watched the six kids as they laughed and rolled around on the mostly dry grass.

Autumn straightened from the shallow trench where she was carefully dropping peas exactly four inches apart, just like Nancy told her to. "I think I will too."

"The first year is the hardest." Nancy went back to gently covering the peas Autumn so carefully placed.

REGRET

The women spent the past week digging up a garden plot in Autumn and Jerry's backyard. The family lived in town in an old two-story that still had beautiful wood trim and even a couple stained glass windows. It made Nancy wish her house had just a little more character, but that wasn't what her old farmhouse was built for. It was built for purpose, not beauty. A purpose it served quite well over the years.

Nancy was barely done covering half a row when a familiar voice hollered behind her. "Hey Nancy."

Nancy waved at her longtime customer as the woman passed by, walking her tiny puffy dog. "Hi Betty. How's it going?"

"I'm ready for some market shopping I can tell you that." Betty waved again. "See you soon."

Betty was the fifth person to interrupt their work this afternoon. Living in the country her whole life meant people passing by and stopping to chat was a new sort of experience for her. It was something she never considered, since moving was never a thought that crossed her mind. At least not until she saw the beautiful home Paul lived in and the amazing kitchen he used to make cold sandwiches.

Nancy squatted back down to continue covering the peas. "Do you like living here, in town?"

Autumn was a full row ahead of Nancy at this point and still dropping shriveled hard peas into the chilly ground. "It's really convenient. There are other kids around for the boys to play with." She looked over at Nancy and gave her a grin. "It gives me a little break."

"I can imagine. I only had to keep up with two and I was ready to lose my mind frequently." Nancy stood up and scanned the bed. "How much do you guys like peas?"

Autumn glanced over her shoulder. "Is this going to be a lot?"

Autumn managed to drop three long rows before Nancy realized how far along she was. "It will be quite a bit."

"Oh." Autumn stood up, looking at the rows herself. "I guess we will learn to really like peas."

"Well, you could can them or you can freeze them." Nancy stretched her back, trying to relieve the tightness of working in the garden all week. Her body wasn't quite back in the swing of things after the winter.

"Or, I would be happy to trade you if there is something I have you would want. I can always sell peas at the market." Peas were one of the first crops to come in the spring and Nancy's customers were always chomping at the bit for fresh produce after the long winter.

Autumn smiled, showing off her dimples. "You are the best, you know that?" She stepped over the planted rows and wrapped one arm around Nancy's shoulders. "I really am a little jealous Mina and Beth get you as a mother-in-law."

Nancy squeezed Autumn back. "Let's call you an honorary then."

"Moooooommmmmm!" Autumn's youngest son fell down on the grass holding his stomach.

Nancy started across the yard. There were no other kids around him and nothing to explain why he appeared to be in agonizing pain. His little face was crunched up and he was rolling from side to side, his arms wrapped around his belly.

"Is he okay? I didn't see what happened." Nancy turned to look for Autumn, assuming his mother would be running along beside her. She wasn't. Autumn was finishing up in the garden, sliding mounds of dirt over the pea trench.

"He's fine."

Nancy kept moving, a little disturbed at Autumn's lack of concern. She reached his side and went to her knees, inspecting his little body for injuries. "What's a matter honey?"

The little boy groaned dramatically. "I am soooooooo hungry."

"Told you he was fine. He does this every day before breakfast, lunch, and dinner." Autumn hollered over her shoulder as she kept moving down the last row, not even looking up until she was finished.

Nancy looked down at the starving child before her. "Is your stomach eating itself?"

His brown eyes shot wide. "Can that happen?"

Nancy laughed and sat in the grass beside him. "No silly boy." She started tickling him. "You scared me to death, you know that?"

He laughed as he tried to squirm away from her. "Stop Miss Nancy. I'm sorry."

She relented, shaking her head as he jumped up and ran away.

"Nana?" Kate's voice came from the side yard where she and Liza stood, transfixed, staring across the street at the parking lot that served the downtown businesses.

Nancy shoved her achy body up off the grass and went to see what they were staring at so intently.

Kate raised her arm to point at a small rental car parked beside one of the many landscape islands placed throughout the large lot in an attempt to beautify the chunk of blacktop. A man jumped out of the passenger door to help a woman hastily approaching with her arms full of grocery bags. "Is that the lady who looks sorta like you, 'cept her face is frozen?"

Nancy watched as Carol shoved her plastic shopping bags at the man. He struggled to grab them all from her, barely managing to hold them all before she waved her hand in his face and walked to the driver's side, leaving him to wrestle open the trunk of the small hatchback while balancing an overflowing armload.

Nancy squinted at the man, trying to get a better look at him. A baseball cap was pulled low on his head and large, dark sunglasses covered a good portion of his face making it nearly impossible to get a good view. Still, there was something oddly familiar about him.

"Yes sweetheart. That's Nana's sister Carol."

"So that's her." Nancy hadn't even heard Autumn walk up beside her. She stood with her arms crossed tightly over her chest, a scowl on her face.

Nancy blew out a loud breath as the man climbed in. Carol didn't even give him time to shut his door before the car started pulling away, his right foot still on the ground. "Yup."

"Who in the heck is that dude with her?" Autumn watched as the car sped away.

Nancy shrugged. It would appear Carol already found a new man to do her bidding. One more check in the 'Carol hasn't changed' column. It was filling up significantly faster than the 'Carol is different' side.

"That is crazy." Autumn dusted her hands on her already dirty jeans. "Did you figure out why she's here?"

Nancy shook her head. "Not yet."

****

Paul pulled into the Wal-Mart parking lot and shut off his truck. Walking quickly through the parking lot, he grabbed a basket as he entered the fluorescent lit store.

Now that everything was out in the open between him and Nancy, it felt like a weight was lifted off his shoulders. The cloud that hung over his head so many years finally evaporated, letting the sun shine through.

For so long he'd only focused on the things he wasn't. The ways he was lacking and unfortunately the relationships he'd had only reinforced his insecurity. But everything felt different now. Now there was someone who said he was enough.

Every broken bit of him.

Now it was time to start showing Nancy what he could offer her instead of worrying about what he couldn't.

The first stop was electronics. The end cap had the newest releases making it easy to find a chick-flick she hopefully hadn't seen before. Then wine.

After adding a bottle each of mid-priced red and white he found a couple kinds of cheese and a variety box of crackers to go with it. Now all he needed was something sweet. The cookie aisle was a dangerous place for an already hungry man to be and by the time his basket hit the check-out conveyor belt it was overflowing with sweets. Only part of them for tonight.

The young girl scanning his items smiled at him. "Looks like you have a nice night planned."

"I guess we'll see." Paul paid for his groceries and was back on the road with the cashier's words still rolling around in his head.

'Nice'. She said he had a 'nice' night planned. That one word was enough to make him double-back to the same old insecurities and just what he couldn't give.

Paul set his bags on the passenger seat and pulled out of the lot, mad at himself. He hadn't even made it an hour before the thoughts easily ran back to the front of his mind.

Was this something he would ever be able to get beyond?

Maybe Nancy was telling the truth. Maybe it didn't matter to her. But it mattered to him. More than it probably should and certainly more than he wanted it to.

He wanted to enjoy every second of his time with Nancy. He'd dreamed about it for years and now that it was happening, the idea of spending it obsessing about what he couldn't give her was starting to piss him off.

The truck turned onto his street and he saw her before the tires hit the driveway. Nancy was sitting on his porch, a book on her lap and a shopping bag at her side. The sound of his truck tires squealing on the fresh layer of blacktop that was put down in the fall snapped her eyes off the pages.

She stood up, a beautiful smile spread across her face. A smile for him. Maybe even because of him.

By the time he was making his way up the front walk with two bags in one hand and his keys in the other, she was holding his storm door open.

He wrapped his arm around her waist and pulled her in for a kiss. "You're early." He kissed her again. "And at the wrong house."

She giggled as she continued to press her lips against his, her eyes open. "Sorry. I just thought it made more sense for me to come to you."

He tipped his head to the side, and looked down at the bag in her hand. "And you brought…?"

She held the bag higher. "I made some snacks."

"You're crashing my party." He slipped his key in the lock and twisted open the door, letting her slide in before him.

Nancy looked over her shoulder at him as she made her way toward the kitchen. "I had some spare time so I thought I would put a few things together." She set the large brown paper shopping size bag on the counter and started pulling out containers and lining them up across the granite.

He watched as the line of food grew to include a smallish container of some sort of dip with a bag of chips, a divided tray of vegetables already cut, deviled eggs and a very large box of both cookies and brownies. Paul raised his eyebrow at her.

"What?" Her eyes were open wide, an innocent look on her face.

"But did you bring wine?" He lifted both bottles out of his bag.

Nancy laughed and started fishing through his remaining plastic bags, adding his purchases to the food she brought. When it was all laid out, she turned to him. "I don't think we have to go out to dinner."

Paul wrapped her in his arms, looking down into her upturned face. "How am I supposed to take care of you if you won't listen?" He'd been very clear about his plans for the night. He wanted to come get her and go out for a nice dinner. After all the meals she'd made for him, it was time to return the favor.

Nancy fingered the button at the collar of his shirt. "I suppose I'm not really good at being taken care of."

It was no wonder. She'd done the taking care her whole life. First her dad and younger sister after their mom died, then

Thomas and Rich, now she was trying to lump him into her comfort zone. He wasn't going to have it.

"You're going to have to get over that."

"I suppose I can try." She gave him a sly smile. "But only for you." Her hand gently grabbed his where it rested on her hip and pulled it up. "How's your hand. Should I have carried you into the house?"

She kept a straight face for less than two seconds before bursting into laughter, throwing her head back as she cackled at her own joke. It was infectious. This was the woman he'd waited for. The funny, witty, kind and caring woman he'd loved nearly his whole life.

Nancy wiped at her eyes. "I'm sorry." She cleared her throat and blinked a few times before giving his hand a once over. "It looks better."

Paul opened and closed his fist a few times. "It feels better I think."

It had been nearly a week since that night and his memory was no clearer than before. Who he had actually seen, if anyone, was still a mystery and unless someone came forward to accuse him of giving them a right hook, it looked like it would stay that way.

Nancy started loading her arms with the food. "Can we eat on the couch while we watch that?" She nodded to the movie on the counter.

"We can do whatever you want." Paul grabbed the remaining items and followed behind her, setting his armful beside hers then going back to the kitchen. "Do you want me to open the red or the white?"

Nancy stood by the couch pondering for a second. "I think white." She started laying out the food while he fished through the kitchen drawers trying to remember which one he kept the corkscrew in. By the time he found it, she'd wandered back into the kitchen.

"I saw the weirdest thing today while I was at Autumn's." Nancy set a stack of lids beside the sink and leaned against the counter, her arms crossed over her chest, watching him struggle with the foil covering the cork. "You don't have to pull that off. It will open anyway."

Wine wasn't his drink of choice so opening it was not a skill he'd honed. "That is good news." He screwed the device into the cork through the foil. "What did you see that was weird?"

Nancy shook her head and raised her eyebrows as if the disbelief still hadn't worn off. "I saw Carol out shopping."

He glanced sideways at her while trying to gently coax the cork from the bottle. "I've only seen part of the woman's wardrobe and I know that's not weird. She probably shops daily."

"That wasn't the weird part." Nancy took the corkscrew from his hand and began twisting the cork free giving him a free hand to hold her glass in one while he started to pour with the other.

"There was a man with her." Nancy's brow furrowed. "He seemed familiar, but I'm not sure why."

The wine bottle crashed at Paul's feet, the heavy glass breaking into a few pieces and clear liquid pouring over his shoes.

Nancy looked at it, then at him. "Red's fine."

TWENTY-TWO

PAUL GRABBED HIS travel mug from the holder attached to the dash of his truck and tipped it back adding another swig of coffee to the belly full of scrambled eggs and bacon Nancy made him for breakfast.

If she kept going the way she was, and he hoped she did, it wasn't going to take him long to get spoiled. Sleeping with her at night, waking up to her in the morning. After just a few nights, he almost couldn't remember what it was like without her waking up next to him.

And he didn't want to.

His life was everything he'd always wanted it to be. The woman he'd always loved beside him, loving him back, giving just as much as she got, maybe even more. It should be perfect, and it almost was.

There was only one problem. One nagging memory he just couldn't seem to shake that was only spurred on by Nancy's offhand comment about seeing Carol with a man. A familiar man.

It wasn't possible. People didn't just come back to life. He knew Sam was dead, he'd seen the gravestone that marked where he would've been if there'd been anything left of him in the car that night, but until he knew what really happened at the bar and who Nancy saw Carol with, there would be a shadow clouding his time with Nancy.

Sam successfully tainted most of Paul's life but the pecker sure as hell wasn't going to haunt the rest of it. So he made an excuse about going to check on the house he and Mina just finished and left Nancy to relax while he went to find out what in the hell was going on.

Hopefully he had better luck than everyone else since no one had been able to get a straight answer out of Carol since she showed up less than a month ago. The woman was dodgy and acted hell bent on worming her way back into Nancy's life for whatever reason.

He was going to find out that reason.

The first stop was to figure out where Carol was staying. The options in a small town were pretty limited. Not too many people came here for recreation so the need for hotels was low.

It took less than five minutes to cruise through the first parking lot. Unless Carol switched rental cars, she wasn't there.

An hour later Paul was pulling out of the last lot, still without a clue as to where Nancy's sister could be staying. He assumed it was early enough in the day that most people would still be in bed, but maybe Carol was an early riser and was already gone for the day doing whatever a non-working, hotel dwelling, husband steeling, child abandoner did.

Paul pulled to a stop at a red light, tapping his fingers on the wheel. Was he crossing a line by doing this? Technically, this might not be any of his business, but when it came to Nancy his boundaries were always on the blurry side. That's how he ended up sending the local dentist more than a few repair jobs over the years. When it came to her, he just didn't know when to back down.

He sat, waiting for the light to change, trying to decide if he was crazy or paranoid or both, when he heard a woman's loud voice in the car beside him floating through the open window along with the warm morning air.

It was difficult to make out her words over the sound of his truck's engine, but the voice was unmistakable. He knew it was Carol without looking, which he did anyway.

She was in the driver's seat, giving the person in the passenger seat hell over something. Her head was bobbing around on her neck, making the perfectly flat hair on her head swing around like she was in a wind tunnel.

Paul leaned closer, trying to look past Carol but the height of the cab of his truck compared to the lowness of her rental car kept him from seeing anymore than the other person's knees. Just as he was about to unbuckle and scoot across the seat, Carol's car made a right on red, leaving Paul to squint at the quickly disappearing two door.

"Damn it." He was so close. All he needed was to see the face on an unknown man in that seat and this stupid wild goose chase he was on would be over.

A horn honked behind him. The light was green and he was still staring at the ass end of Carol's car.

Pulling away from the light, he turned right at the next intersection. Maybe if he hurried he could cross their path and run back into the twosome. Not literally.

Unless it was Sam in that seat.

That's why he was almost sure he was crazy. There was no way it was Sam. Carol probably brought a man back with her and just didn't want to spring her strained family situation on him. It made sense. Much more sense than the idea that Sam somehow survived the fiery crash all those years ago.

But he had to be sure. Until Paul saw this guy, face to face, with his own eyes and it wasn't Sam, well... He wished he hadn't quit drinking. Again.

His foot eased off the accelerator as the next crossroad came into view. Paul craned his neck to the right, hoping to see the little white coupe, zipping along. Nothing. It took three more empty intersections before he could admit defeat.

Wherever she'd gone, Carol went there quickly because it was like that damn little white car just disappeared into thin air. Hell, maybe Sam was a ghost. Maybe they both were.

He turned the truck around to go back and check on the house so his excuse to Nancy wouldn't end up a lie. It needed to be walked through anyway. An empty house was a dangerous thing to have sitting around. Hopefully it would sell quickly because his time was about to be split two very important ways. Thomas' house and his Nan.

And she *was* his. And he protected what was his. That's why it was so important for him to figure out what Carol was up to before the woman could have a chance to hurt Nancy again. Unfortunately, he didn't have any more ideas on exactly how to accomplish that.

By the time the house came into view, Paul was beginning to realize he needed help if he was going to get to the bottom of this, however, the top of his list of potential cohorts was a woman who might not be so quick to go behind Nancy's back.

Then he noticed the car in the driveway and realized he may not need that help after all. There sat the white two-door he'd seen just a few minutes ago. The same white two-door he'd tried so desperately to find. It looked like it found him first.

Paul pulled into the newly widened driveway and parked next to the empty car, peering in the windows as he climbed out of his truck. All that was inside was a handbag on the passenger seat and a few sheets of folded paper in the center console, most likely the rental agreement.

He squinted up at the house then scanned the empty yard. Where in the hell were they and why in the hell were they here? His suspicions of Carol and her motives for being here were growing with each passing minute. There was only one reason for her to be here.

Snooping.

The irony of her snooping on him as he was attempting to snoop on her was more than irritating so he decided to ignore it. He knew his motives were good, maybe not for her, but her motives? Questionable at best.

"Hey Paul." Carol appeared around the side of the house, stepping carefully in the newly sown grass, attempting to keep her pristine, suede heels out of the dirt.

REGRET

"Carol." He kept his eyes locked on the side of the house she emerged from, waiting for the mystery man to appear behind her. "You here alone?"

Her eyes almost imperceptibly widened. He would have missed it if he wasn't so damn suspicious of everything the woman was doing. "Yes."

He cocked his head at her. "Why?"

She smiled at him, continuing across the driveway toward him. "Why am I here or why am I alone?"

"Why are you here?" He tried to keep his voice calm, even though he wanted to scream at her, make her tell him why she was here.

And who was here with her.

Carol looked over her shoulder at the house. "Nancy told me you and Mina fix up houses and I wanted to come see your handy work."

He continued to stare at her. There were few words he had to say to her, even fewer he should say in the presence of a woman. Even one like her.

Carol cleared her throat and licked her lips. "How are things going?"

"Fine." He narrowed his eyes at her. "How are things going for you?"

She smiled widely. "Wonderful. I'm so happy to be back home and back with my family." She took a few more steps his way. "And my friends."

"Maybe you could show me through your house." The smile was still on her face as she continued to advance on him, swaying her hips as she walked. Just as her hand was about to land on the front of his shirt, he turned away.

"Yeah, I don't think so."

****

Nancy turned her key in the ancient front lock of the old farmhouse door, twisting it a little to the left before making the full clockwise turn to unlock the deadbolt, just as she had her whole life.

She walked quietly into the home she'd worked so hard to make her own. It had been days since she'd been here and it was starting to make her feel guilty. Like she was abandoning an old friend.

It used to be one of her favorite places to be, the house where she grew up, where her own sons grew up. But recently those feelings changed. Maybe it was time to consider moving on. Maybe not just moving on but also moving in. It might be time for this house to be a safe haven for someone else.

Because Nancy might have found a new home. One that felt like it was made just for her.

There was something about Paul's house the minute she stepped inside. It felt warm and loved and happy. She still loved this old house, but that was where the old her thrived, safely wrapped up in her own little world. Alone.

It was time to add another change to her list.

Nancy wandered through the front room. The house was filled with so many memories, most of them good. It was the last place she saw her mother and her father.

And Rich.

Nancy stopped at the shelf that held her most prized possessions. Pictures of her mother when she was healthy and happy. The faces of two sweet little boys with matching gaps where their front teeth should be, smiled out at her from a homemade frame. Nancy touched the faded paper, still held firmly in place by a pile of cracking glue.

Next to it was a tiny clay pot, pressed into shape by small fingers to hold her rings while she did dishes. She picked up the small blue painted bowl and tipped it over, gently rubbing the pad of her finger over the initials etched into the bottom in careful block letters. RD.

Richard Dalton.

A tear carefully edged its way out of the corner of her eye and slowly made a path down her cheek. She was such a fool. So unwilling to see what was going on around her that her sister could even name her son after his father and Nancy would never make the connection.

Sam Richards. Richard Dalton.

That poor little boy never had a chance. Two parents who were out for one thing and one thing only. Themselves. How could a child overcome that?

He couldn't. Even with a mother who loved him like her own and a brother who would have gone to the ends of the earth to help him. It wasn't enough. There was nothing that would have been.

That would be the hardest part about leaving this house. It was where all the happy memories of the little boy Rich were created. Those days of a sweet little boy, running around the backyard playing with his brother were how she was going to choose to remember him.

Letting go of everything else would be difficult, but it was time. Time for another fresh start for their family. First Thomas, now her, hopefully soon Beth.

Nancy stopped midway to the kitchen. Beth.

She turned slowly, looking around the house as the idea circled her mind, picking up momentum as it went.

REGRET

Maybe Beth would want to live here.

Nancy couldn't stop smiling as she tossed her dirty clothes into the washer and went upstairs to pack a fresh bag to take with her to Paul's. Her new home that held her new life and the promise of happiness.

Nancy set her open bag on the bed and began filling it with enough necessities to last a few days. As she crossed to the closet to grab a few blouses, her toe caught on a box sitting by the dresser. A box that had been sitting in that same spot for months, waiting for her feel ready to open it again.

It was the same box that brought Rich so much pain. She'd been so afraid it would do the same for her that it sat untouched. Nancy knelt beside it and opened out the flaps.

There were hundreds of letters from a grown man to a girl who was barely eighteen. A girl who also happened to be his wife's sister. What had Sam said to make Carol willing to risk everything to be with him?

Or was it the other way around?

This box might hold the answers she had no luck getting out of her sister, even all these years later.

Nancy picked up one of the envelopes. It was yellow and crisp around the edges from sitting quietly in the attic for the past few decades. Carol's name and the address of the farmhouse were scrawled across the front in Sam's handwriting.

She slipped the letter free and unfolded it before she could change her mind. It was time to stop avoiding what happened. It wouldn't change anything. But it could at least let her know the truth about her own life. Nancy scanned the single paper.

Sam spent the entire page confessing his undying adoration to his teenage lover. Begging her to keep seeing him. He would do what she wanted. He would do anything to be with her.

Nancy tossed it on the floor and grabbed another. More of the same. Undying love. He would do what she asked of him as long as she swore to be with him. Blah, blah, blah.

Nancy rolled her eyes. How did she not see what a schmuck Sam was? Here was a grown man who sounded like a lovesick kid, begging to have his love returned. It was ridiculous.

Nancy thumbed through and scanned a handful more before she couldn't stand it any longer. From the letters it seemed as if Carol tried to break things off and he was devastated, chasing after her like a lost puppy. It was nauseating.

Nancy stood up and started to pile the letters on the floor back into the box when something caught her eye. It was another envelope addressed to her sister in Sam's handwriting. It looked exactly like the others. Except for one thing. It was mailed from California.

Three months after Sam died.

TWENTY-THREE

NANCY SPED DOWN the road, her hands gripping the wheel, her mind racing. There was no way.

No freaking way.

Was this even possible? There was a headstone for Christ's sake. A grave. She'd been there many times in her weaker moments to spit on it. That meant he had to be dead. Yup. Died in a fiery single car crash.

So fiery, there was nothing left.

Shit.

Nancy wiped one hand down her face as the reality of what might have actually happened started to really sink in. In his letters, Sam said *'I'll do what you want'*. Surely it wasn't what she was thinking it was.

What kind of man would fake his death to leave behind a wife and two kids?

The answer only helped bolster her suspicions.

The same kind of man who would cheat on his wife with her sister.

Nancy squeezed the steering wheel until her knuckles turned white. If Sam wasn't really dead, he would be soon. Lucky for him that would mean he and Carol could be together forever, just like he wanted.

Because Nancy was going to kill her next. If she could ever find her.

She'd been looking for an hour. Carol wasn't at the hotel where she was supposedly staying and Nancy hadn't seen her car as she did a sweep through downtown. Now the sun was going down, making it significantly more difficult to identify who was driving any small white car that passed her on the road.

She was on her way back home to get those fucking letters and go back to Paul's. If there was anyone who could help her right now it was him. Even if all he did was help her regain sanity just enough to be less intent on committing a murderous rampage.

Nancy crested the little hill just before her house. The blinding light from a pair of headlights still on bright filled the car interior. She squinted against the glare, but it still penetrated enough to cause flashing blind spots big enough she almost couldn't tell it was Carol passing her.

Had she been at the farmhouse? Nancy laughed.

The bitch was probably coming over to see what else Nancy had that she wanted. So far at least she hadn't gotten anything worthwhile. Especially if she was still the proud owner of Sam Richards.

If he was the man in the parking lot with Carol the other day, maybe he was enjoying a fate far worse than death. The thought brought Nancy no small amount of joy. Imagining Sam following her sister around like a puppy dog as she berated him. Hell, she didn't have to imagine it. She might have seen it with her own eyes.

Nancy could feel the heat burning her cheeks as anger, or maybe rage was more like it, took over. In her whole life she'd never felt like this. Out of control. A little crazy.

And giddy.

She couldn't wait to see their faces when she found them. The jig was up and it was time to pay the piper.

Carol was going to have to answer every question Nancy had whether it was at her hotel room or the place where they grew up. Then she was leaving and Nancy didn't care if it was back where she came from or off to jail. As long as she was out of

Nancy's life and away from everyone she loved. This was ending now. All of it.

Nancy pressed on the gas, clearing the short distance left to her house in seconds, her blood pumping in her ears, the anger building at an exponential rate egging her on.

The farmhouse came into view. Nancy spun her car into the driveway and threw the little four-door in reverse, missing the gear in her haste. She couldn't move fast enough and it was causing her to be careless. Nancy leaned back against the seat's headrest, taking a slow breath. Now was not the time to lose her mind. Now was her chance to even up the universe and she owed it to herself and Rich to do it right.

It was time to hunt down the woman who ruined their lives. And ruin hers back.

As Nancy's foot hit the gas to back out, a shadowy figure darted away from the backside of the farmhouse and into the darkness of the fields surrounding it.

Two red lights flickering down the long lane in the distance on her left snagged her attention. It was an access road, more of a path really, that Thomas, and her dad before him, used to get the tractors around the fields. And for some reason, now Carol, in her small white hatchback.

What in the hell was going on and who the fuck was in her house?

Nancy sat for a minute and tried to decide what to do. Carol and whoever was with her were up to something and from what she suspected they'd done all those years ago, the two of them were capable of very bad things.

And it appeared she might be their target.

Shutting off her headlights, Nancy slowly backed out of the driveway, keeping her eyes peeled for any more suspicious figures loitering on her property as she drove back the way she'd come, making it to the spot Carol turned off the road in less than a minute. It was time to find out the truth about both her past and the present, and chances were she would find it down that drive.

With the fields still empty from the fall, there was no way she could follow Carol in her car without being seen and heard so Nancy pulled off the dark, isolated road, parking her car in the field, hoping she was as much out of their sight as they were out of hers.

She switched off her interior lights before opening the door and stepping out into the darkness, the soles of her lace up work boots sinking into the well-worked soil.

The field was barely visible, lit only by the dim rays coming from a crescent moon. The almost complete darkness would work in her favor, making it easy to cross the field without being seen as long as she was quiet and stayed low.

Nancy carefully shut her door, pushing gently with her hip until the latch clicked, holding it closed. She started the long walk back to where Carol's car disappeared from sight. She was halfway across the large field before her sister's car came into view. The little hatchback was still lit up, parked between the front field and the back field, tucked into a grove of pine trees.

It was awfully arrogant to be sitting in a place you shouldn't be, doing things you should not, in a car that was shining like a beacon. It took one hell of an ego to do something like that.

Or two hells of egos.

The lights of the car suddenly shut off. Nancy moved a little slower, listening to the sound of her own footsteps across the soft dirt while still keeping an ear out for whoever was in that car and whoever was at her house.

She cut a wide path to the left, hoping the trees would provide a little cover. Just as she reached the far end of the tree line, a car door shut. Loud enough it would seem the person closing it thought they were alone in this field.

They were wrong.

"Did you get them?" Carol's voice was sharp, cutting through the silence with its hard edge.

"They were all over the place." The man's voice was older and rougher, but still unmistakable. It was a voice Nancy would

321

have never guessed to hear again. Not even in her wildest dreams. Or nightmares.

It was the voice of a dead man.

Nancy moved closer. She needed to see him. See his face.

Carol was barely visible in the moonlight walking away from the car toward Sam as he finished the trek across the field to her car, holding something.

Nancy crept through the trees, moving quickly from one to the next and squatting down behind the trunks as she tried to gain a better view of the scene unfolding before her.

By the time Carol yanked the item from his arms Nancy was close enough to see his face, half of it black and blue, along with exactly what her sister was so interested in. It was the box of letters.

"I don't understand how you could forget them before." She walked to the car and opened the trunk, shoving the box in. "I gave you a list for Christ's sake."

Sam's eyes shifted around as he followed her to the back of the car. "Didn't you hear me? I said they were all over." He leaned in close. "She read them."

Carol's eyes narrowed as she glared at him. "What do you mean, she read them?" Carol shook her head. "No. She said Rich is the one who read them."

Sam took a step back. "They were in her room, in a pile on the floor. Some of the letters weren't even in the envelopes anymore."

Carol yanked the trunk back open, the light illuminating her actions as she flipped open the box and began pulling out the loose letters. The letters Nancy sat on her bedroom floor reading less than two hours ago.

"Goddamnit Sam." Carol shoved the papers back in the box and slammed the trunk for the second time. "You are such a fucking waste of my time." She gave him a hard shove. "I should have left you to rot when your daddy's money ran out."

Carol walked back to the driver's side of the car with Sam on her heels. "I'm sorry. I didn't mean to. You can fix this baby. You can fix anything remember?"

He was like a kicked dog. Still coming back for more love. Begging her sister's forgiveness just like in the letters. Nancy felt sick to her stomach.

All these years she thought it was Sam.

Carol opened the door and reached in. "For once you're right. I can fix anything." She reached into the console area and stood back up her arm outstretched, the barrel of a revolver pointed squarely at Sam's face.

Sam's eyes went wide as the color drained from the uninjured side of his face. He slowly raised his hands. "What are you doing?" He started walking backward as Carol began to advance on him. "I'm sorry baby. I didn't mean to forget them."

Carol continued to follow him, holding up the very familiar looking pistol. "You never mean to do anything. You didn't mean to forget the letters. You didn't mean to marry Nancy. You didn't mean to get her pregnant. You didn't mean to screw up the crash."

"But that was okay. You fixed it baby. Just like you fix everything. You'll fix this too." Sam was moving faster now, his voice becoming more desperate as his eyes flashed around in the dim light from the car's overhead light, still activated by the door Carol left open.

"What do you think I'm doing now? I'm fixing it." Carol straightened her arm, focusing her aim.

Sam was at the edge of a wet weather creek bed that cut through the farm. He glanced behind him as he teetered on the edge. "We'll get the money. She's stupid. You'll get her to believe you and then we'll be in."

Nancy stood up and walked to the car. Carol was about to be very pissed and she wanted to watch every second of it, front and center.

"No. *I'll* get the money. *I'll* be in. You'll be gone. For real this time."

Carol cocked her head to one side. "Bye, bye Sam."

Nancy could hear the smile in her sister's voice and it sent chills down her spine. Never in her wildest dreams would she have ever guessed her sister was a psychopath. A bitch, yes. Selfish, yes. Even a sociopath, but never like this. Carol was a monster and Nancy was glad her father wasn't here to witness just how depraved his youngest daughter was. It would have broken his heart.

Nancy heard the gun in Carol's hand make a clicking sound. Then another. Then three more in quick succession.

This time it was Nancy's turn to smile. She reached into Carol's rental car and twisted the headlights on, illuminating the tragedy playing out in the moonlit night.

Carol spun around, the disabled gun still clutched in her hand.

Nancy gave her a little wave. "Hey Carol. How's your night going?"

Her sister froze, her mouth hanging open.

"Nothing to say? That's weird." Nancy walked around the door, toward her dead husband and cheating sister. "Cause you were feeling pretty chatty a few seconds ago."

Carol narrowed her eyes and pointed the gun, their father's gun, at Nancy.

REGRET

Nancy laughed. "You just tried to shoot that thing like five times. It doesn't shoot Carol. I had them all disabled when I started watching the girls." More accurately when Liza figured out how to pick the lock on the gun safe.

Carol gave her a little grin. "You mean my granddaughters?"

Nancy's face went cold. Suddenly all her focus went back to her original plan.

She was going to kill Carol.

Nancy started running toward her. It was one thing to steal her husband and fake his death, but if she thought for one second she would take those little girls away—

Lights flashed across the field and an engine revved as a vehicle plowed toward them. Nancy looked up to see a deep orange flash as it zoned in on Carol, her hand still pointing the gun at Nancy.

Nancy ran toward her sister, this time not intent on beating her to death with the pistol. She hit Carol full speed, knocking her flat on her back and out of the way of Paul's GTO.

Nancy heard the engine rev again and rolled off Carol just in time to see the look of terror on her former husband's face as he was caught in the beam of Paul's headlights.

Paul hit the gas again making the motor roar, the sound echoing through the field. Sam turned and started to run with Paul hot on his heels.

Carol was wheezing beside her, trying to regain the breath Nancy knocked out of her during the takedown. Nancy stood up, not really sure what to do, watching as Sam scrambled across the uneven ground. She gasped as he lost his balance and fell face first into the dirt. The GTO slowed down, giving Sam time to get up and start running again.

Nancy breathed a small gasp of relief. If Paul wanted to hit Sam, he would have done it by now. Instead, he was simply chasing him through the field as his old high-school buddy ran in circles, screaming his head off.

"He's going to hit him!" Carol started to get up, her eyes glued to Sam as he ran through the field.

Nancy turned to her sister in completer disbelief. "You were just going to shoot him." She reached out just as Carol was almost back on her feet and shoved her face first back to the ground. Hard.

Nancy sat on Carol's back, one leg on each side of her shoulders and fished her cell phone out of her pocket. She dialed Thomas' number. The police would have to be her next call. She needed someone who could get here fast.

Before Paul ran Sam to death.

TWENTY-FOUR

NANCY OPENED THE door to her new home just as the only man who'd ever really loved her came up the sidewalk, his hair still dusty from working on her son's house. "Hey handsome."

Paul gave her a smile as he swept her into his arms, giving her a drywall dust scented kiss. "Hello sweetheart. How was your day?"

He kicked his boots off onto the tray beside the front door as she shut it behind him. "It was good. I got most of the market set up and made a pie."

She followed him as he made a beeline into the kitchen he'd so lovingly crafted, always with her in mind, even if she didn't know it then.

Right after Carol and Sam were arrested, Paul insisted on moving her into his house. It was an excuse with them locked up, she was the safest she'd ever been, but he jumped on it, insisting he just didn't feel safe knowing how easily they were able to get inside her house.

She could have told him the locks were never changed as long as she'd lived there and Carol still had a key, but she didn't want to. She wanted to be here. With him. Laughing as he searched like a madman for the pie she made him for dessert.

"You need to take a shower first anyway." Nancy turned him by the shoulders in the direction of the stairs. "I will get dinner on the table while you do that." She smacked him on the butt as he walked off, the slap of her hand making him jump as he grinned over his shoulder at her.

She watched him disappear and went back to the kitchen. Just as she was stirring the basil into the spaghetti sauce, her cell phone rang from the counter beside her.

She picked it up and tucked it against her shoulder. "Hey honey."

Paul wasn't the only one who'd been a little paranoid lately. Thomas called her at least twice a day every day since she'd found Carol in the field trying to frame her for Sam's murder so she could step into the vacancy Nancy's absence would leave. And the inheritance she thought she would then be the beneficiary of.

Carol planned to make their family's money her next pile of cash to blow through. Turns out Nancy's sister was quite the financial swindler with Sam's parents as her willing and completely informed accomplices.

Because they'd known all along that Sam was still alive.

Collected the life insurance he took out with them as the beneficiary and sent it straight to where he and Carol were living commitment and responsibility free on the other side of the country.

Then they croaked and left her all their money too.

All so their precious angel baby could live the life he deserved.

Too bad for Carol their own dad wasn't a generous toward her. And why would he be? Nope, Jim Dalton did the right thing and left everything to his beloved grandsons. That was a fun day. Watching Carol discover she would never have gotten a dime of their father's estate. No matter who died.

"How are you?"

Nancy smiled. "I'm fine. Just like I was three hours ago when you called."

"That's good. I just wanted to let you know we got those locks replaced and the motion lights installed on the farmhouse."

"Who's we?" Nancy stopped stirring the sauce.

"Don helped."

Nancy smiled. Maybe no one else understood little Donnie Jenkins, but she did, and it did her heart good to see her son giving him another chance. "I'm glad."

"It was a little bit of a hard sell, but Mina finally caved. I had to bring you into it. I told her you felt bad for him."

"I do feel bad for him. Not everyone is like you Thomas. Not everyone knows their worth." The kid had a hard life and was just trying to find his way. Now he'd lost everything he'd managed to scrape out from the horrible life he was given. It was all gone. His job, his home, his reputation. She wanted something good to come of all that happened and maybe helping Don would be it.

"Well, we'll see. As long as he stays in line and helps get the work done, things will be fine." Thomas sounded unconvinced.

"Things will be better than fine. I promise." Nancy heard Paul's heavy footsteps on the stairs. "Honey, I've got to go. I'll call you tomorrow so we can set up a time to get Beth moved in."

Given all three options, Mina's house, the new house being built or Nancy's place, Beth chose to move into the farmhouse and Nancy couldn't be happier. Now that no one could argue about the security there, it would be the perfect home for Beth and the girls.

Paul wrapped his arms around her waist as she set her phone back on the counter. "That smells good." His voice was low and growly in her ear as he nipped at her neck.

Nancy smiled as the hair on the back of her neck stood up and her belly flipped. As worried as he was about certain things being an issue, the man had been more than able to make up for what he perceived as his shortcomings.

She let her head fall to one side as he continued teasing the sensitive skin of her neck with his tongue. "You taste so good."

She giggled. "Hopefully dinner will taste better." She tried to scoot away from him to dump the pasta into the pot of boiling water. He grabbed her by the hips and spun her to face him.

Her legs clenched together when she saw his face. A level of intensity she'd never seen before filled his darkening eyes. "I'm not hungry for dinner right now."

She swallowed hard. "You're not?" Her voice was hoarse.

He shook his head. "No."

Paul dipped his head and covered her lips with his. Nancy whimpered into his open mouth. This was so unlike him. Normally Paul was sweet and tender, but the man pressing his body against her now was passionate and... and...

Hard.

"Oh my God." Nancy whispered against his mouth as she felt a rush of wetness join the ache building between her legs.

Paul's hands were scraping up her shirt, dragging the fabric over her head. He grabbed the straps of her bra and pulled them down her arms, exposing her tightly puckered breasts, leaving the black lace garment dangling from her ribcage. With a frequent audience, she'd taken more interest in her undergarments.

He undid her pants and shoved them down before wrapping his hands around her waist and dropping her bottom on the granite counter top, the cool rock chilling her heated pussy.

His mouth covered her breast, raking the sensitive tip with his teeth while he kneaded the other nipple between his calloused fingers. Her head was swimming, the passionate way he was acting and the possibility of having him inside her making her dizzy with need.

"Paul. What—" She gasped as he nipped at her breast just as he slid two fingers inside her body. "Oh my God." Her head fell back as he continued to stroke her, both with his mouth, and his hand.

The second his thumb touched her clit, she felt her thighs begin to quake. "Paul, I'm going to--"

He pulled his hand off her body. "Not yet baby." She heard a zipper raking open. "Not like that anyway."

He pulled her legs around his waist. She moaned as she felt the thick tip of him pushing into her. She felt his eyes watching her intently as he slowly pressed his dick deep inside her, inch, by agonizingly pleasurable inch. When he was completely buried within her, he growled against her ear. "I don't know if I can hold back."

She opened her eyes, staring into his dilated pupils. "I don't want you to."

And he didn't.

She moaned as he began to move. It had been so long since she'd had a man inside her she'd almost forgotten how good it felt. The fullness of his body, stretching the tightness of hers, rubbing against places inside her in a way nothing else could.

Her hands clenched at the edge of the counter as he fucked her, sucking hard on her nipples as he groaned her name.

"You feel so good baby." He moved faster, his dick becoming even harder, pushing even deeper.

She grabbed at his shoulders as she began to come, the feel of his mouth on her and his cock inside her too much. The ringing in her ears almost drowned out the sound of her screams as she came harder than she ever had.

With one last impossibly deep thrust, Paul moaned into her breast as he filled her, finding his own completion.

Nancy slumped forward against him panting. "What in the hell was that?"

Paul nuzzled into her neck. "If you don't already know, I'm not going to be the one to tell you."

"I mean, you said…" She tried to string a coherent sentence together, but was struggling to organize her thoughts. "I thought you couldn't do that."

Paul leaned back, his face nonchalant. "Turns out there's a pill for that."

Nancy wanted to slap him. "You mean you hadn't already tried that?"

Paul shrugged.

"You're a pain in the ass you know." What kind of man doesn't go to a doctor for something like that?

One like Paul.

She shook her head at him. "Pain in the ass."

He grinned at her. "And I'm all yours."

Thank you so much for reading Regret!

If you loved it and want to know more check out my website at www.janicemwhiteaker.com

for all the latest news.

You can also join my readers group on Facebook to get the first peek at covers and exclusive excerpts you won't find anywhere else.

Hopefully I'll see you soon!

xoxo,

Janice

Made in the USA
Middletown, DE
02 August 2025